The Faulty Endearment

Breanna Cropp

The Faulty Endearment

First Edition: 2022

ISBN: 9781524318055
ISBN eBook: 9781524328115

To the guy who inspired the villain,
you know who you are, and you know
what you did.

Table of contents

Prologue

Two men rushed into the room, "Sir, we may have finally found the right person."

The Commander looked over at them, his checkerboard like eyes glistened with delight, "Finally," he closed his book, "we will win this war."

He turned and grabbed a throwing knife from the table and threw it at the prisoner he had been keeping in his office, barely grazing his ear. The prisoner stumbled to the side, his ruby red eyes flickered with anger and fear while one of the guards almost fell over in astonishment.

One of them managed to find their voice, "Sir you could have killed your strongest warrior."

The Commander looked at him, now holding a teapot, "Well it's a good thing I missed isn't it." He poured a cup of tea and offered it to the guard. Nervously the guard took it and drank it. "Good, isn't it?"

"Very good sir, but what is this after-"

He was cut off by a coughing fit before

falling to the floor grasping at his throat. The Commander leaned down close to his ear and whispered, "I never miss," before the guard collapsed completely. "Now," he said, turning to the other guard, "Plan the attack and capture of this person." He turned around. "I need to speak with this one." He looked down at the prisoner.

The prisoner looked at The Commander and stood up, "Strange how you want to speak directly to me now, you've only had me in here for a week now."

"You will hold your tongue if you don't want another scar like the one on your face."

The prisoner closed his mouth immediately, "As you just heard we will be getting a new warrior soon, I need you to make sure they won't step out of line."

"What are you so worried about?" The prisoner followed The Commander with his gaze, "You mentioned a war. Since when were we at war?"

"Oh, we're not yet but we will be as soon as we capture the one I sent the guards to find."

"What is this about, why are you after an innocent?" The prisoner was getting aggravated.

"Calm yourself Aiden!" Aiden backed off as if he had not been called by that name in a long time, "Now this person is not innocent, this person is going to destroy this kingdom I've built, your home."

Aiden looked away, "They will want to destroy this place." He looked at the floor with a conflicted look in his eyes, "We must eliminate them. I cannot allow anyone to destroy the only place I've ever called home."

"That's a good warrior. Now go back to the palace and keep order amongst your subordinates."

Aiden nodded and left. As he left The Commander got a good look at the burn on his left shoulder blade. It was an insignia of a rose with two swords stabbed through the bud with a banner that had 'A19902' written inside, the brand of a warrior. With that brand they couldn't leave and if they somehow managed to, they would be found in a week at most. The writing in the banner was different for everyone, easier to keep them in line that way.

"Good luck. Your kingdoms will soon fall," The Commander walked over to the dead guard and took a picture out of his pocket and examined it, "See you soon, Princess," He tossed the picture in the air and threw a knife, nailing the picture to the map, "I can't wait to meet you and take you home," The Commander laughed deviously.

Chapter 1

A breeze swept through the open window as birds chirped playfully outside. Juniper stood up and walked out onto her balcony.

"Another beautiful day in the kingdom," she said to herself.

"Still talking to yourself I see."

Juniper yelped and turned to see her lady-in-waiting Melanie.

"Melanie, you startled me."

Her smile always lit up the room around her, always with her optimistic attitude toward life she always did know how to see the best in others. She walked over to Juniper's closet and took out a dress. She had beautiful brown eyes and her long rich chocolate brown hair was tied back in a ponytail.

"Okay Your Highness your parents need you in the throne room soon." She brushed the skirt down with her hand, "They said you needed to meet with someone."

"You say that like you know who it is."

Juniper and her lady-in-waiting both laughed and she got ready for the day. Juniper was never told who she was meeting; she guessed that Melanie didn't know either. Juniper sat down in front of her vanity and watched as Melanie did her hair. Juniper had brilliant green eyes and sandy blonde hair. She, like every royal, had powers but hers were a bit different. Among five kingdoms there were five royal families, and each had powers, the royal family of Flora had nature related powers, the royal family of Vulcan had fire powers, the royal family of Oxidane had water powers, the royal family of Aquilo had air powers, and finally the royal family of Terra had earth and rock powers. Juniper was the princess of Flora but her powers weren't limited to plants; she also had an unusual ability to heal and could summon things to herself no matter how far away. She was the most skilled with her plant powers as there was nobody who could really train her other powers. Melanie finished her hair and Juniper got up and began walking to the throne room, as she walked through the halls, she couldn't help but wonder who this person was or why they might be visiting her kingdom.

She arrived at the doors to the throne room and took a deep breath. Juniper opened the doors and saw three people: two were her parents, the king, and queen of Flora, and the third was the older brother of one of Juniper's friends. He was the prince of Aquilo. He had pale skin and black hair and his eyes were a shimmering gray like storm clouds. He always walked with confidence and was always ready to help others. He was always there when someone needed help but he didn't trust non-family easily, he was someone you could talk to about pretty much anything but he didn't like to talk about his problems if you hadn't earned his trust.

"Juniper." Her mother spoke first, "I believe you know Prince Aeolus."

Juniper smiled and curtsied, "I have had a few conversations with him yes."

"Hello Your Highness." Prince Aeolus said with a bow.

Juniper's father looked at the prince then to Juniper, "You two are going to spend the day together."

Aeolus looked at the king, "May I ask why? I was also never told why I needed to come here, to begin with."

Juniper looked at her father as well, "I have the same question."

The king looked at his daughter and the visiting prince from his throne, "We are still working out the kinks in this plan but as soon as we finish you will be told."

"Very well your Majesty," The prince turned to Juniper, took her hand, and gently kissed the top, "Well Princess, if I must spend the day with someone, I'm glad it's someone as beautiful as you."

"Should we be leaving now, dad?" Juniper asked.

"Yes please. Have a nice day." The king said with a smile.

The prince and Juniper turned and left. When he kissed the top of her hand, she remembered how much of a charmer Aeolus had been in school, he was almost two years older than his sister. He had a lean muscular build and was about six foot five. He was twenty years old and when he was in school, girls were trying to earn his favor: every day he would find a declaration of love in his bag or one time he found a note from a secret admirer in his dorm. He never could figure out how they got in. Juniper knew for a fact that a few particularly strange girls had small shrines to him, and unfortunately his sister Elaine had to share a dorm with one of them. This girl always begged for Elaine to set her up with Aeolus, but Elaine always said no. Juniper pondered whether or not she should tell him. He looked like he was lost in thought, so she decided against it. They walked in silence for longer than Juniper was comfortable with, luckily Prince Aeolus became uncomfortable as well, as he was the first to try to break the tension.

"You have a lovely palace."

"Oh, um thank you, it was built using my family's powers, so it's got a lot of nature inside and out."

"I see they made the windows using big translucent leaves."

"Yeah, they do a really good job at letting light in while keeping the elements out," Juniper stopped and looked at one, "They do really add to the aesthetic of the palace as well."

Aeolus looked at them and smiled, "Yes I suppose they do."

Juniper and Aeolus continued with their small talk, even in the life of royalty not much had been happening in either kingdom. They made it to the doors of the courtyard and stepped outside into the lively garden of Juniper's palace, the pathways were well kept as always, and the archways looked as elegant as ever. The flowers grew not in neat rows but instead how you would see them in a meadow, there were fruit trees and vegetable gardens. The guards often allowed some wildlife to nest and create homes as long as they weren't disrupting day-to-day life indoors which for the most part they didn't.

As they walked Juniper saw a baby fox that had been injured, she gestured for Aeolus to stop. Aeolus stared at the fox pup with a confused look like he couldn't figure out how it got in. Juniper took a few careful steps toward it, got on both her knees, and held her hand gently out to the pup. The pup nervously walked toward her and sniffed her hand. After deciding Juniper was safe it allowed her to pick it up. Tenderly Juniper picked up the pup and did her best to heal it. She did better than she normally would. The fox pup leaped to the ground and wiggled happily. Just then its parents showed up, the mother fox walked over, picked up her pup and bounded into the undergrowth of a tree and the father fox followed. Juniper smiled and stood up and met the eyes of Prince Aeolus who had a surprised look in his eyes.

"You healed that fox pup?"

"Yes, I've had unusual powers all my life."

Aeolus looked like he wanted to question her further but before he could a palace guard came and told them that they were needed in the throne room. They walked through the halls in silence once again. Juniper looked at the prince and he seemed anxious to learn why he was here to begin with. They got to the throne room and Aeolus opened the doors for Juniper. They walked in and Aeolus was taken aback to see his parents and sister in the throne room. Elaine looked incredibly nervous.

Aeolus looked at them, "Mom, dad, what are you doing here?"

As soon as Juniper registered who they were she swiftly curtsied, Aeolus's mother smiled and spoke, "We were further along in this process then we realized, lucky for us you two didn't leave the palace."

"Pardon me, Your Majesty but what exactly is happening?" Juniper asked, relatively confused.

Elaine smiled and laughed in an awkward way, and her father put a hand on her shoulder, "We'll tell you two over dinner. We needed you here to tell you to be in the dining hall at six, we're also not quite done."

Juniper looked at her parents who nodded at them, "You two should stay together for the rest of the day." said Juniper's mother, "Elaine why don't you join them."

Elaine looked at her brother then to her parents, who gave her a look that clearly asked ''can you keep a secret for one day?' She nodded and walked over to Juniper and Aeolus. As they walked out Juniper saw confusion and a bit of sorrow in Aeolus's eyes. He didn't trust a lot of people, but he could always trust family but now it seemed like his trust had been shattered. Elaine was terrible at lying; it was one reason Aeolus could trust her, no secrets in his family. She had the same shimmering grey eyes as her brother, but her hair was a golden brown. She always knew how to break tension or make someone laugh. When she walked into a room people noticed, much like her brother she got love confessions every day, but nobody ever snuck into her dorm and left a secret admirer note. She was also really bad at hiding her feelings, Juniper could tell she was nervous and wanted so badly to tell them what they were talking about in the throne room. Finally, Juniper couldn't take the silence anymore and broke it.

"So, Elaine, have you gotten any messages from the rest of our friend group?"

"Actually, yes Victoria wanted to hang out, she also wanted me to ask you, Silvia, and Hazel to join us but I forgot." Elaine chuckled.

Aeolus scoffed, "I don't get why you're being so secretive today," He stopped and looked Elaine dead in the eye, "I know that you know why we're here, why can't you tell us?"

"Aeolus, I'm sorry but it's not my place to say." She looked away like she couldn't meet his gaze.

"I thought I could trust you, but then you

can't tell me something that pertains to me."

"Um If I may." Juniper said, "This does pertain to me as well Aeolus."

Aeolus looked at Juniper, "What are you suggesting?"

"That we wait, they said they would tell us."

"Please Aeolus, I want to tell you I really do but I just can't."

Aeolus turned away, "Fine, but if we're not told I swear, Elaine."

Elaine grabbed her brother's shoulders, "I promise."

They spent the rest of the afternoon talking about local politics and news in the kingdoms of Flora and Aquilo. They also tried their best to avoid talking about the reason the royal family of Aquilo was visiting to begin with. Aeolus talked about what he had been doing while Juniper and Elaine were still in school. Soon six o'clock rolled around and it felt like time flew by faster than normal because Juniper, Elaine, and Aeolus had done a good job keeping themselves distracted. They made their way to the dining hall. Elaine seemed happy, probably because the secret would finally be out, while Juniper and Aeolus were nervous to discover what this secret was. Juniper opened the door to the dining hall to see both queens and both kings already there waiting patiently for their children. Juniper, Elaine, and Aeolus all took their seats without saying a word. As soon as they sat down their parents exchanged a look.

"Okay." Juniper's father started, "I know you two are anxious to know what's going on."

Aeolus and Juniper looked at each other before Aeolus's father cut in, "We wanted to tell you sooner, but we had to wait until we were confident this would work, and now we are."

"So, what is this plan?" Aeolus asked,

Aeolus's mother sighed, "We've decided to unite the kingdoms of Flora and Aquilo."

Juniper looked at them with a guess at what this could mean but still needing confirmation, "So what does this mean? Why couldn't you tell Prince Aeolus and me?"

Juniper's mother spoke up, "As Prince Aeolus is the future king of Aquilo and you Juniper are the future Queen of Flora, in order to unite the kingdoms," She looked at the prince then back to the princess, "You two will need to be married."

That took Juniper and Aeolus by surprise, Juniper froze in her seat while Aeolus looked like he wanted to shout but had lost his voice. Elaine sighed; the weight having been lifted off her shoulders.

Aeolus managed to find his voice but couldn't

think of anything to say when his father spoke up again, "I know this isn't ideal for either of you however," he waved his hand, "This will be good for both kingdoms."

"I don't want this to come off like I don't like Prince Aeolus but, this sounds a bit rushed don't you think?"

Juniper's father looked at her, "We've actually been planning this for a long time."

Aeolus looked at them, "How long?"

Aeolus' father spoke again, "Two years. We started planning this after you graduated and were waiting for Princess Juniper to graduate before we told you."

Aeolus looked away again, and Juniper was speechless. Juniper wanted to leave and get her mind straight but she couldn't leave without asking first. However, her father understood her facial expression, "If you need a moment, you two can leave."

At first, Juniper wasn't going to leave, but Aeolus got up and walked out so Juniper followed. She closed the door behind her and looked around to see Aeolus walking down the hall to find a place to think; Juniper thought about following him but decided against it as seeing her might make him feel uncomfortable. Instead she went down to the courtyard, found a bench and sat down. She thought about what this would mean, and time passed without her even releasing, it turned out she had sat there for the entire evening.

Melanie walked up to Juniper, "Your Highness, you should probably begin heading to bed."

"W-wait what time is it?"

"About nine-thirty"

"Wow, I was out here for a long time."

"I'm not surprised, the news about you marrying Prince Aeolus was a bit startling for me as well."

"I'm not really sure either of us are ready for that," Juniper shifted in her seat uncomfortably, "I mean I just graduated and I'm only eighteen and he's twenty and our parents want us to get married so soon?"

Melanie chuckled, "That's tomorrow's problem, right now you should be more worried about getting a good night's rest."

"Yeah, you're right, I'm tired anyway." Juniper stood up and stretched, "See you tomorrow, Melanie."

Juniper went to her room, took a quick shower, brushed her teeth, and got dressed for bed. As Juniper climbed into bed, she looked out her window and couldn't help but wonder what her future held. Juniper tried to sleep but couldn't. Eventually she grew tired of tossing and turning so she walked out onto her balcony.

Whenever Juniper was upset, or she felt like her world was unbalanced she would go to the courtyard or out onto her balcony to listen to the wind blow through the plants and to the nocturnal creatures that were out and about running along tree branches and calling out to each other. Right now she really felt like she needed to get away and just listen to nature. As Juniper stood on her balcony, she felt the brisk cool night air press against her arms, there was a gentle breeze that blew occasionally. Juniper didn't know whether Aeolus' family had gone home yet, but someone showed up to tell her.

"Crazy day, huh?" Juniper jumped back and looked over to see Prince Aeolus floating next to her balcony, "Oh I'm sorry I didn't mean to startle you, Princess."

"It's fine, I didn't know you were still here."

"Yeah, I thought you knew but I didn't go back to the dining hall and by the time my parents found me sitting alone it was too late in the day to go back to Aquilo," Aeolus glanced around "May I come onto your balcony?"

"Oh yes, I didn't realize you were still keeping yourself up."

"Yeah." he landed on the balcony, "But again today was wild, wasn't it? I mean I wasn't expecting to end the day finding out I was going to be engaged to a princess as beautiful as you."

"I bet girls at school would be so jealous." Juniper said looking to Aeolus, "I mean so many of them liked you."

"Oh yeah like the one who managed to break into my dorm room."

"Or the ones who made shrines to you."

"Wait, people actually did that?" Aeolus got a surprised look in his eyes, "I thought that was just a rumor!"

"Nope Elaine had to share a dorm with one of them."

"Gah, I feel so bad, I wish I had known."

Juniper and Aeolus looked at each other and laughed, they hadn't ever really talked like this. While they talked, they didn't use titles, just their names, they let go of their worries and almost forgot about how broken up they were earlier. In the middle of their conversation, a bird swooped behind Juniper with a loud cawing noise which startled her so badly she fell forward right into Aeolus.

"Oh my, I'm so sorry."

Juniper tried to push herself off him, but he wrapped his arms around her. He was a good foot taller than her, "No you're staying here."

Juniper looked to the side and saw the sun rising over the horizon, then something fell on her head. She glanced up and realized that Aeolus began resting his chin on her head. She smiled, wriggled free from his arms and stood proudly in front of him with her hands on her hips.

"Rude. I was enjoying having a chin rest!"

"Well, then you'll have to find a new one."

Aeolus looked down at Juniper, with the sun still peeking over the horizon bathing everything in a golden light. Aeolus leaned forward and kissed Juniper. As they stood together, she took his hand, and he gently touched her face. To Juniper it felt like all time held still, there was nobody else around and she felt safe. When Aeolus pulled away Juniper opened her eyes and saw him smiling down at her, her face still cupped in his hand.

"I need to go back to my room before my parents wake up and find me missing," he said jumping up onto the balcony railing, "See you soon, Princess."

As he flew down through the window of his room on the wind, she stood there the feel of the kiss still tingling on her lips.

Chapter 2

Juniper walked down to the dining hall for breakfast, as she walked in and saw she was the only one there. It wasn't unusual for her to be the first one there so she just took her seat and waited patiently. After about five minutes her parents came in to see her waiting for everyone.

"I wasn't expecting to see you this morning after the events of last night."

"Marcus!" Juniper's mother scolded.

"Well, am I wrong, Alice? She did seem awfully upset."

Juniper laughed, "I'm fine really I am." She looked at her parents, "It just took us by surprise is all."

Her father smiled, "Got my looks and your mother's personality."

"Oh, I'm sorry I should have taken after mom in looks. That way I actually would have turned out good looking."

Queen Alice snickered, and King Marcus rolled his eyes, "Low blow."

As they continued talking Elaine walked in, "Hey I got messages from Victoria saying she got Hazel and Silvia to meet her at a cafe in her kingdom and wants us to join her!"

"Sweet, did she give you a location?" Juniper asked.

"Yes, she sent me the location in case we choose do join them."

"Princess Elaine will your parents and brother be joining us for breakfast?" asked the Queen.

"Yes, they will be."

Just as she said that Aeolus entered and bowed respectfully to Juniper and her family, "Good morning Your Majesties." He looked to Juniper, "And good morning Your Highness."

Juniper smiled, "Good morning to you as well Prince Aeolus."

"Why are you two being so weird?"

They all waited patiently at the table with a bit of small talk to keep them occupied while they waited for the visiting king and queen to arrive for breakfast. When they did, they spent the beginning of the meal in silence before conversation started once again.

"So have you two calmed down about the arrangement?" asked Aeolus' father.

Aeolus and Juniper looked at each other before coming to a silent agreement, "Yes, we have, dad. The news just caught us off guard."

"Good now Elaine, and Princess Juniper, I know you plan to go out with friends today, you may tell them but only as long as word doesn't get out. We are doing a press conference tomorrow about this." The king looked and his daughter and Juniper "Understood?"

"Yes, dad."

"Understood Your Majesty."

The rest of the meal was silent again. Soon the meal was over and the Royal family of Aquilo went back to their home while Elaine and Juniper left to meet their friends. As soon as they arrived at the cafe they were swarmed with paparazzi and interviewers. Lucky for them there were three other princesses there so guards quickly took over, but Juniper heard one of them shout something interesting.

"Princesses, can either of you update old rumors that say one of you is in a relationship?"

Juniper knew better than to respond to any questions from the press or paparazzi and Elaine did too. They both simply smiled and waved as they entered the cafe, usually this was the most popular cafe in Vulcan but because there were five princesses here and one of them had an overprotective father, the cafe was pretty dead.

They walked in and were greeted by an overly

happy girl with blonde hair and blue eyes, "Junie! Elaine!"

"Hey Silvia." responded Juniper

Silvia was a happy bubbly girl with pale skin and ocean blue eyes and was the princess of Oxidane. She tended to walk around spreading happiness to whoever she talked to. Silvia led Juniper and Elaine to a table with their other friends Victoria and Hazel, Victoria was a confident girl and pretty sporty she had dark brown hair and heterochromia, one eye was yellow and the other, orange like flames. As she was the princess of Vulcan, she also had darker skin. Hazel was more of the shy type. Her father was a bit overprotective. She also had dark skin but lighter than Victoria's. She had black hair that faded into brown with dark brown eyes. She was the princess of Terra.

As Juniper sat down, she started a conversation, "You will not believe the weekend we had."

Hazel looked at them, "What do you mean we?"

"Both Elaine and I had a strange weekend."

Victoria rolled her eyes, "You're not the only ones. I mean come on have you met my brothers?"

She sat back in her chair and crossed her arms, "I was out riding, and they insisted on coming. I didn't want them too but then..." Victoria said, starting a long rant about how her brothers ruined her ride by scaring her horse then accidentally burning theirs. "I mean can you really beat that?"

Juniper looked at her then looked at Elaine and they both stifled a laugh, "Oh I think I can top that, Victoria."

Hazel looked at Juniper, "Are you sure? I mean Victoria's seems pretty hard to beat."

Juniper shrugged and that sparked Silvia's interest, "Something happened." She looked Juniper dead in the eye, "Spill!"

Juniper took a deep breath and looked at Elaine who gave her a look that said, 'you tell them.' Juniper looked over at them, "So I found out that my parents and Elaine's parents were planning..." Juniper looked around to make sure nobody was listening. When she was sure, "To have Prince Aeolus and me get married."

Silvia shot to her feet, Hazel almost screamed, and Victoria fell over.

"What!? Married? You and Prince Aeolus!?" Silvia said, unable to form complete sentences.

"Shh, not so loud Silvia." Elaine said sternly, "We got permission to tell you and only you, this will be revealed to everyone tomorrow during a press conference."

"Who's having a press conference?"

"Yeah, who's having a press conference?"

The group of girls turned to where the voices were coming from and saw two boys that looked a lot like Victoria except one of them only had yellow eyes and the other had orange. They were Victoria's younger brothers.

"Damian, Lucas, what are you doing here?" Victoria asked her brothers.

"We followed you here." Damian replied.

"Do mom and dad know this?"

Lucas smiled up at her, "Nope, but we'll be sure they blame you for taking us with you without permission."

Damian giggled, "Now about this press conference-"

Victoria cut him off, "It's a press conference with our favorite music artist James Mousai, the one you don't like at all, now I don't know how you got here but go home."

"But Victoria."

"NOW!" Both of the twelve-year-old boys sighed and left, and Victoria composed herself and asked, "Junie, have you ever been to a press conference?"

"No, but you and Silvia have, any tips?"

Silvia thought for a moment, "Prepare yourself mentally, and be very careful with how you word things."

Victoria nodded, "It's like the press except you have to respond, not just pose for the camera and it's like ten times more intense."

"We'll be there if you want us there for support." Hazel added, "But I will not be going on stage."

Elaine laughed "You won't have to Hazel."

Somehow one of the journalists managed to get inside the cafe and started bugging the princesses, trying to get a scoop.

"Hello, Your Highnesses, I'm Sadie Cooper and everyone is dying to know if any of you are in a relationship?" The reporter asked in a kind of annoying tone of voice.

Victoria rolled her eyes, "Guard! Please escort Miss Sadie Cooper away from us."

"No please, I need this scoop." She cried out as a guard removed her from the cafe.

"We should probably start heading home, considering that if one of them managed to find her way in the others are going to find a way in as well." said Juniper.

"Yeah, we probably should," replied Hazel, "See you soon to hang out?"

Silvia nodded, "Definitely."

The princesses said their goodbyes and returned to their respective kingdoms. Juniper went to the courtyard after she got back to the palace and sat down to listen to the animals play and the leaves rustle. Silvia told her to be prepared mentally so that's what she was doing. She felt a presence walk up to her but couldn't tell who it was because her eyes were closed.

"Hello Princess, I'm glad to see you back from the café."

"Oh, hello Melanie," Juniper looked at her, "Again with startling me."

"My apologies Your Highness."

"Would you like to join me?"

"What are you doing?"

"Just listening to the garden' it's quite relaxing."

Juniper sat back and closed her eyes, and Meline sat down next to her and closed her eyes as well. They sat in silence for a while. Juniper couldn't tell how much time had passed but one of the maids came by and told the princess dinner was in five minutes.

"Well, I should head down there then."

Melanie stood up, "That was more enjoyable than I thought it would be."

"We should do it again sometime then."

Melanie went about her business and helped clean, while Juniper went to the dining hall. When she arrived, her parents were already there having a pleasant conversation.

"So then I-" her father said, cutting himself off as she walked up to the table.

"No, please don't stop on my behalf, what did you do?"

"Junie don't tease him for forgetting."

"Ha ha, very funny," her father said in a sarcastic tone.

Juniper and her mother laughed as Juniper took her seat, "So how many people are going to be at this press conference?"

"Hmm due to this being some big news from two royal families you can count on a lot of people wanting pictures and for you to answer their questions," said her mother

"Yeah, it's like walking on a minefield, especially this one as it will be broadcasted live to all five kingdoms." Her father continued, "make sure you look nice and don't fumble your words."

"Yeah, Silvia said to be careful with wording."

Her mother nodded, "Yes a lot can be taken out of context when you don't word things properly."

"I would recommend using the rest of the evening to get ready."

"I will dad. That's what I was doing before dinner, getting a calm mind to be mentally ready for that."

After that, the rest of the conversation was

normal, with talking about plans for the future and what happened at the cafe with the random reporter who found her way in. They all had a good laugh about that. After the meal ended Juniper headed up to her room to prepare for the press conference. She found a decent dress with a matching pair of shoes, she showered, did her normal skincare routine, and was ready to sleep by nine-thirty.

She went to sleep and when she woke up the next morning, she felt refreshed and ready for the press conference. Juniper grabbed an apple out of her fruit bowl, ate it then got ready for the press conference. She did her hair and makeup, got dressed, and put her shoes on. She decided to go simple with basic makeup, a braid that wrapped into a bun, and a simple yet elegant off the shoulder pastel greenish-blue dress with matching flats. Juniper walked down to the throne room and saw her parents talking with the castle steward to make sure everything would run smoothly while they were gone for the day.

"Ah Junie, good you're ready." Her mother said, turning to her as the steward left.

"Yup let's go."

The family walked out and got into the car to head over to where the press conference was being held. As they arrived there were a ton of reporters and photographers, she heard reporters shouting questions asking what this was about. There were a few people asking for autographs from the royal family, however, they were all kept behind dividers to allow the royals a clear path to walk. There was a gap between two of the dividers and a little girl fell through it. Juniper walked forward and offered the girl, who looked about nine, a hand to get up.

"Are you okay?"

"Um, yes." the girl said before looking up to see who had helped her, "Y-you're the princess."

Juniper smiled, "Yes I am." she leaned down and whispered something into the girl's ear, "Want to see something cool?"

The little girl's eyes widened with excitement, and she nodded vigorously. Juniper held her hand above a crack in the asphalt and a daisy grew into her hand. Juniper picked the flower and tucked it behind her ear. The girl felt her accessory and saw her notepad and pen on the ground, she swiftly picked it up and offered it to Juniper to ask for an autograph. Juniper took and signed the note pad. The girl thanked her and ran back into the crowd. Juniper looked at her parents who smiled knowing that was the perfect reaction to what happened. After they walked in, they saw the royal family of Aquilo already inside.

"Hello Your Majesties." Elaine said as she curtsied

Aeolus looked over and bowed his head in greeting before turning back to the window. To Juniper he seemed nervous, not that she could blame him, she was too. However, Juniper curtsied in greeting to his parents.

"Good morning, Your Majesties, how are you?"

The king looked at her, "Although I shouldn't be, I was surprised at the amount of people who showed up just to witness our arrival."

Juniper noticed too, "I suppose you're right there was definitely more then there usually is when one of us goes anywhere."

Juniper's mother shrugged, "It shouldn't be all that surprising considering the fact that two royal families show up for a press conference together, it's a pretty big deal."

"Well for my brother and my friend it is." Elaine said.

Juniper looked over at Aeolus again and saw the tension in his shoulders and stance. She wanted to talk to him but before she could someone came into the room and told everyone it was time to begin. They were lead out to a stage set up for with name plates telling them where to sit. Unsurprisingly they had Aeolus and Juniper sit next to each other. As the two families walked on stage to take their seats, cameras flashed, and people started asking questions immediately.

Juniper's father picked up a microphone "Please hold all questions until we are seated and ready to begin."

They all took their seats and the questions started again, one reporter who Juniper remembered was the first to get an answered question, "I'm Sadie Cooper and my question to you King Marcus is why is this press conference being held?"

"An excellent question Ms. Cooper," said the king, "This meeting is being held to reveal some incredible news."

"And what is this news Your Majesty?"

"I will hand this question off to Prince Aeolus." Juniper's father looked at him and he froze.

Juniper knew what to do, "This news is that Prince Aeolus and I are going to be married."

Questions erupted from the crowd after a brief gasp from every person in the room, and the tension in Aeolus's shoulders released a bit. She knew that when he got nervous he froze up and couldn't speak, she didn't want him to be embarrassed like that on live T.V. He looked at Juniper with a look that said thank you before turning back to the crowd a bit more relaxed and starting to answer questions. The rest of the press conference consisted of questions about wedding plans and plans for the future. The press conference ended pretty quickly for Juniper, afterward she managed to actually talk to Aeolus.

"Hey, are you okay, you seemed really tense?"

"Yeah, it was just nerves I guess." He looked at his hands, "I'm fine now."

Juniper's mother called her over and she turned back to Aeolus, "See you later, yeah?"

"Of course, Princess."

Juniper walked over to her mother, "Yes mom?"

"We are heading home now."

Juniper and her parents went back to the kingdom, and she spent the rest of the day relaxing. She was reading a book in her room when she heard something outside her window. She walked out onto her balcony and called out,

"Hello, who's there?"

When she got no response, she figured it was just her imagination but when she turned around, she saw a pair of checkerboard eyes with hair to match. The person looked down at her with a huge smile on his face, but it was not a happy smile.

"Hello Your Highness."

Juniper looked at him, fear flooding her face, "Who are you?

"You'll find out in time but for now-"

He cut himself off by punching her in the face, nailing her in the eye socket. She tumbled backward into the railing and knew she would fall if he hit her again. She didn't know how to fight but he struck her again this time in the crown of her head knocking her out cold. He picked her up, leapt off the balcony into the courtyard and vanished with a flash of light.

Unaware of how much time had passed she was awoken by an intense burning feeling in her left shoulder blade. Soon the pain became unbearable, and she slipped back into unconsciousness. After several hours she woke up in a strange room wearing a white shirt and jean shorts with black combat boots and a black jacket. She looked around and saw the man who brought her here standing in the corner of the room.

"Hello, glad to see you finally woke up from your slumber J49825." he said, with a smile.

"Who are you?" Juniper asked.

"Just someone who wants to talk. Not here and not now. You'll find me again, but for now enjoy your new home, my warrior."

He vanished from the room again and she

was left alone in the dark. The room shook and lit up so brightly she closed her eyes and when she opened them again the room had changed to more of a bedroom type space in which she was left to her own thoughts when a girl walked in with violet eyes and dark skin with even darker hair.

"Hello, what are you doing in my room?"

"I don't know."

Chapter 3

The girl looked at Juniper with confusion and for the first time in a while Juniper didn't know what to do. The girl seemed to be wearing a similar outfit to Juniper but she was wearing white leggings underneath her shorts, her jacket was tied around her waist, her shirt was cropped with short sleeves, and she had a silver pendant hanging from her neck. Juniper tried to get up but that must have startled her because she shouted at her.

"FREEZE!" The girl shouted, and Juniper froze in place.

She walked around the edge of the room to a small desk keeping her hand up and palm open toward Juniper. The girl opened a drawer in the desk and took out a sheet of paper and read it, she sighed and lowered her hand and Juniper fell to the floor.

"Ow." Juniper said, getting up, "How did you do that?"

"It's my power."

"I thought only members of the five royal families could have powers."

"Well, my rank does say I'm queen, but my blood line is not royal."

Juniper looked at her, sizing her up, "What kingdom are you from?"

"Um this one," She glanced down at the paper "now J49825."

"Juniper, but Junie is fine if that's easier"

"Okay Junie, so you have powers too." She sat down on the chair, "What are they?

"Um, you don' already know?" Juniper asked, "Do you know who I am?"

"Not a clue, why? Am I supposed to?"

"Yes, I'm a part of the royal family of Flora," Juniper answered, bewileded Erica didnn't know that.

She seemed to take that as a joke before standing up and gesturing for Juniper to follow. Reluctantly she did, Juniper followed the girl into a small room when she turned around and faced Juniper.

"Good luck, you'll need it."

"What, what's going to happ-"

Juniper got cut off by the door closing and the room shifting around her. The walls fell around her allowing her to see where she was. She was standing in the center of an arena and looked around to see the girl that brought her there shuffling through the crowd to a spot next to a strange boy but before she could get a good look at him, she was tackled and pinned to the ground. Juniper didn't know what to do so she defaulted to immobilizing her opponent. She opened her hands and laid them flat on the ground summoning vines to bind the person on top of her. Juniper got to her feet and looked around to see everyone staring in awe like nobody had been able to do that before.

She heard something behind her, so she whipped around and attempted to summon what they were holding and found herself in the possession of a Basket-hilted broadsword. Unfortunately she didn't know how to use it but the opponent who had been holding it didn't know that. She assumed she was holding it correctly due to the look of fear on his face. She took a careful step forward and lunged but she didn't use the sword. Instead, she grew some leaves and quickly covered her hands and summoned some cacti, which she threw at him. He dodged and so she manipulated the leaves on her hands to wrap tightly around in a mitten type form and summoned some bull nettle and smacked him in the face with it. He stopped and felt his face.

"What did you just hit me with?"

"Um a bit of bull nettle."

"What will it do to me?" He looked up at Juniper, feeling the spot she smacked him.

"It won't kill you." Juniper replied, breathing heavily.

"What will it do?"

Juniper thought for a moment, "It will cause intense dermal pain, burning, itching, cellulitis, and allergic reaction."

He looked at her with concern,

"I-it's okay though I know how to get rid of it."

Juniper looked at the crowd who looked back at her in astonishment, she removed the leaves from her hands and summoned some aloe vera plant, broke it and dabbed it onto the place where she hit him. That's when she felt a breeze over her back and realized a section was missing in her clothes on her left shoulder blade. She felt a presence loom behind her and almost punched it in the face, but it blocked it with ease and looked at her like she was a bad grade on a test before pushing her to the floor. She got a good look and realized he was the one girl was standing next to.

"I have never seen anyone overpower those two so easily."

"Really I got the first one off me with no

struggle at all."

"You must have had some type of formal training."

"No, that was the first real fight I've been in."

"Well, it looks like Erica has a natural to train."

"Who?"

He didn't answer the question, just walked away and Juniper got to her feet. She looked around and realized she was alone again. Everyone in the stands had left and so had the people she fought. The boy had said that Erica had forgotten to introduce herself, but Juniper was confused. Then someone showed up to answer her questions.

"Hello again Junie."

Juniper turned around to see the girl again, "Oh hi, um sorry I never got your name."

"Hm I never told you, I'm Erica."

"So, you're Erica, because that guy said-"

"I forgot to introduce myself, well everyone here already knows who I am."

"Could you explain your powers to me."

"Oh, of course."

Juniper then spent the next few minutes listening to Erica explain her powers which were, when she gave simple commands like freeze or sit, kind of like what you would say if you were training a dog and she held her hand up with her palm open then whoever her hand was facing would obey the command.

"Now." Erica said, "Explain your powers to me."

Juniper obeyed, not because Erica used her power as she didn't, but because this was the first time anyone asked. Juniper explained how her family's power plant related and how hers was to manipulate plants and make them grow on command. However, she had a unique ability to heal and could summon things to her, but these powers were not as easy for her to use as the first one due to the fact that there was nobody who could train them. Juniper told Erica how she was mostly self-taught but that she would like to become more skilled.

"Well because of how easily you won that fight you're already pretty high on the ranking system," said Erica.

"Wait, what ranking system?"

"Everyone here is ranked by skill and power, but mostly by skill."

"What do you mean?"

"We are ranked by order of royal titles, the king and queen being the highest ranking and peasants being the lowest ranking."

"So what rank am I?"

"That would make you the rank of Duchess."

She paused "And if I'm remembering correctly that would bump the girl you fought down to Marchioness."

"Okay, so can you train me to use my other powers?"

"I will do what I can," she turned to look at Juniper, "Were you ever taught how to use a sword?"

"No, I was taught how to resolve political conflicts and stuff like that."

"I thought you were because you were able to hold the sword properly to the point you tricked our best swordsman into thinking he would get skewered."

"Who was the guy who came and talked to me after the fight?" asked Juniper, thinking of a quick description, "The one with the ruby colored eyes."

"That's the highest ranked male and normal warrior, Aiden."

"So, he's the strongest one here?"

"Exactly now, we should get to training. You're going to need it."

Erica left and Juniper followed. As they walked through the hallways, Erica told Juniper to walk with confidence always, that way people would be nervous to even think about challenging her. People looked at Juniper with fear and surprise, she overheard a few whispers saying things like *'I can't believe she won so easily'*. Erica walked into a room and Juniper followed. As she looked around, she saw one other person there. It was one of the people she had fought, the one she smacked with a poisonous plant. He glanced over and she realized he had heterochromia, one eye was a yellow green, and the other was more like seafoam green.

"Oh, it's you."

"Carmine, you know she was just defending herself."

Juniper looked at him, "I could try my healing powers on you, if it makes you more comfortable?"

Carmine looked at Juniper, his eyes were focused, but the tones of his voice made him sound more like a big brother then someone who would fight in a war. His caramel brown hair was long for a guy and was tied up in a short ponytail. His white skin glistened with sweat, and he wasn't wearing his jacket. His white shirt stuck to his body revealing a muscular build, not like Aeolus' but more like a movie star.

"You have healing powers?"

"Yeah. They're not as refined as my plant powers but I can use them."

Carmine looked at Juniper warily before

nodding. She walked forward and touched the spot on his face gingerly, he winced as she touched it, but she closed her eyes and focused. After a minute she looked at him again and pulled away from his face. He felt it and looked at Juniper.

"Thanks for that."

"No problem, and for me it looks like I'm improving." Juniper said with a smile.

Carmine nodded and left, Juniper thought he didn't like her, but Erica said something that changed her mind.

"New record, usually if he's not around people he likes then he won't talk at all and especially won't let anyone touch him."

"Really he seemed nice."

"He is just not around new people." Erica shrugged, "My brother is worse though."

Juniper laughed, "How bad?"

"Complete introvert, never starts conversations himself."

After that Erica spent the next couple hours teaching Juniper the basics of combat. She applauded how quickly Juniper picked it up and taught her a few offensive moves.

"You're really good at this for someone who's never had to fight anyone."

"Weird right, I mean this is so invigorating."

"You could try a bit of sword fighting, I'm not

good with swords but Carmine is, I'm sure he might agree to teach you."

"How sure are you?"

"I'm like eighty-two percent sure."

Just then a bell rang, and Erica turned and left.

"What's going on?"

"Lunch, aren't you hungry?"

Juniper nodded and realized she had not eaten anything since the apple before the press conference. They walked to the cafeteria and everyone turned and looked at her. She followed Erica to get some food, people backed up to let the girls through and Erica found a boy who looked just like her, but his eyes were a shade or two lighter than Erica's and he was wearing glasses.

"Hey Eylam, I don't think you have properly met Junie."

"Hi," said Juniper.

But Eylam looked at the ground and mumbled a quiet, "Hello."

"I see what you mean by complete introvert."

Eylam looked down like he wanted to vanish.

Erica laughed, "It's okay, come on. Your rank is prince your second only to Aiden. That's amazing!"

Erica and Eylam started to have a conversation while Juniper looked around and made eye contact with Aiden. Other than his ruby red eyes he had light ginger hair and freckles, he also had a muscular build like every guy in this place, but his build was a bit more like Aeolus' while Aiden was far more muscular than Aeolus, he was very lean. He had a big scar on his face that went down from a little above his left eyebrow down to his jawline. His eyes were intense, and his movements seemed like he was always ready for a fight. He turned away from Juniper and she decided she had been staring at him for too long. Juniper, Erica and Eylam got their food and sat down. As they sat at a table, those who were sitting quickly got up and left.

"So Eylam, what's your power?" asked Juniper.

"I can manipulate time, but instead of sending things through time I send time through things, but it only works on living beings," he replied.

"That's cool."

"Yeah, I suppose it is."

Juniper looked around, "Who are the other highest-ranking warriors?"

Erica looked up from her meal, "The other two girls in the top four are Aanya and Circe."

"What are their powers and rank?"

"Circe is the one you fought this morning. Her power is shapeshifting; she can turn into a phoenix."

She pointed over to a girl who had brown hair with dyed purplish pink in an ombre style with light blue eyes and freckles. She wore a very happy smile and didn't seem at all upset that she was defeated in a fight this morning. She also had a bow with a quiver of arrows slung over her shoulder.

"The other girl, Aanya, holds the rank princess, the second strongest female. She has omnipresence, the ability to be in multiple places at once."

Erica pointed to a girl with long black hair tied up in a ponytail. She was relatively short and had grape purple eyes and was chatting with a boy but was also using her hands a lot in the conversation.

"Who's the boy Aanya talking to?" asked Juniper.

"He is the third highest ranking boy, Zane, he has ice powers."

Juniper looked at Zane. He had pale skin and icy blue eyes but one of his eyes was covered with an eye patch. While Aanya was talking, he watched her hands not her face, but he smiled while she talked. Eventually she stopped and put her hands down and he started moving his.

"Is Zane deaf?" asked Juniper.

Eylam, without looking up replied, "Yes."

"Okay. I guess that makes Carmine the fourth highest ranking boy."

"Correct Junie. You're a fast learner," replied Erica, "Carmine's power is invisibility."

"So how does one move up the ranks?"

"You challenge for their position," answered Eylam

"Like you walk up to the person who holds the position you want and say I challenge you for whatever position they hold and then they fight to determine who gets to keep it," continued Erica.

"Will everyone take it seriously if you say it as a joke?"

Both of them said yes simultaneously. A bell rang overhead, and everyone got up and left. Juniper assumed that they had set mealtimes so she got up and followed them out. Everyone went out to a courtyard type area and Juniper saw someone standing in a spot that was visible to everyone in the courtyard, it was the guy who had brought her here.

"Hello, my warriors," he said, "I would like to welcome our newest recruit, someone who managed to best the old duchess, earning herself the title of duchess on her first day."

People turned and looked at Juniper and a few of them scowled like they had never gotten that before.

"Excuse me Commander, but she should start from a lower rank like everyone else."

"I'm sorry were you not happy with the fact that you got a lower start because you're weak and couldn't win?"

"Fine I'll show you who's weak, I CHALLENGE FOR THE POSITION OF DUCHESS!"

There was a collective gasp from the group and Juniper's wrist was grabbed and she was ushered out by a few people into a room that looked into the arena. But before she could ask any questions they left, and Juniper was forced back into the arena for the second time that day. Juniper looked the girl who had challenged her dead in the eye and saw the amount of sheer anger that girl felt. She walked around the edge of the arena moving like a wild cat stalking its prey. Eventually she lunged and Juniper dodged, and the girl got up and attacked again. Juniper opened her hands up and pinned her down with vines. She tried to free herself but Juniper continued keeping the girl bound. After a few more moments of struggle, the girl went limp. Juniper took a few steps forward and looked at her. Seeing that she had lost consciousness and deciding she wasn't faking Juniper loosened the vines and a few people grabbed the girl and took her to what Juniper could only assume was the infirmary.

"She's gonna come back for you, Juniper," said a voice behind her.

Juniper turned around to see the king, "Oh hello, it's Aiden, right?"

"You're bold for calling me by my name."

"I'm sorry, would you like me to call you something else?"

He looked at Juniper and raised an eyebrow, "You know what, as you are the first person brave enough to call me by my name, I will allow you too." He went to leave, "But make one slip up and you're a goner."

Juniper stood there stunned at what he had just said when Erica walked up to her, "Wow he's letting you call him by his name."

"Yeah, he won't let anyone do that. What *are* you?" asked Eylam who was starting to get real nervous about being around Juniper.

"A really lucky person I guess."

They spent the rest of the day until dinner training and helping Juniper get more skilled in combat. They asked Carmine to teach her how to use a sword and he agreed and taught her the basics of sword fighting. When the bell rang for everyone to go to dinner, the group went to the cafeteria. As they walked in Juniper saw Aiden sitting alone observing everyone but when he made eye contact with Juniper, he turned his attention to his food like it had become the most interesting thing in the world. She noticed he had a cinnamon bun next to his meal on the plate and Juniper's first thought upon seeing it was that maybe he wasn't as tough as he made himself out to be. After Juniper got her food, she decided to be even bolder and sit with him and try to talk to him. She felt all eyes were on her as she walked over to his table and sat down.

"Hello." she didn't get a response, so she tried again, "Hello Aiden."

He looked up, "Why are you talking to me?"

"Because you seem like a person I can talk too."

He poked the food on his plate with his fork, "You're a strange person, you call me by my name, okay, fine whatever, but now you want to and a pleasant little conversation."

"Why not? I don't see a problem."

He scowled, "I do. I don't need these people thinking I'm going soft on one of you."

She decided to try something new: she discreetly moved the dessert from her tray to the table and got up leaving it behind, "Fine I'll leave you to sit in silence and observe."

She walked over to a different table where she

could watch him without him seeing her. He saw the brownie she left at his table and looked around to make sure nobody was watching and took it. As Juniper watched he took a bite out of the brownie and smiled, and Juniper came to the conclusion that he had quite the sweet tooth. He finished the brownie and ate the cinnamon bun right after, and the intense, always ready to fight look in his eyes melted into pure bliss.

"He's a sucker for sweets." Juniper whispered to herself.

After dinner everyone was instructed to go to their room, unfortunately Juniper didn't know where her room was, but Erica helped her out and once Juniper found her room, she was finally able to think about her home. Her first thought was about her parents and how worried they must be but after that she thought about Aeolus and what he must be thinking. She wondered what everyone was doing and wondered how she was going to get home. Juniper had been repressing her feelings all day, she didn't know where she was or how she'd get back. Juniper felt tears begin streaming down her face as she thought about it.

"Make the best of it Juniper," she said to herself, "It can't be all bad right? You'll get home soon."

Juniper drifted into a dreamless sleep and

woke up the next morning to the sound of the meal bell. She left her room and saw everyone walking to the cafeteria. She went with them and ate her breakfast then walked down the hall to continue her combat training when she bumped into Erica but something about her was off.

Chapter 4

Erica turned around and looked at Juniper threateningly, Juniper backed up and Erica grabbed her and pinned her to the wall.

"Who do you think you are?"

"Erica I'm sorry I didn't mean to."

"Quiet, you have challenged my authority, now you will pay the price."

Erica held up her hand and was about to strike Juniper, but Juniper kicked her in the gut with both feet. Knowing how Erica's power worked she summoned some vines and grabbed Erica's wrists and wrapped them around her hands to keep them closed. She looked at Juniper, anger flickering in her eyes, and a crowd started to gather around the two girls. Juniper looked around and saw Carmine toward the front of the crowd but instead of asking for his help she reached her hand out and summoned his sword. Upon getting a hold of the sword she hit Erica with the hilt causing her to back up. Erica got ready to attack again but Juniper stood her ground and swung the sword creating a big cut over the bridge of her nose. Erica stumbled to the ground and felt her face and saw the crimson color on her fingertips and blood trickled down her face and over her lips. Then Juniper decided she needed to finish this fight fast. So instead of using the sword she dropped it and side stepped, grabbing one of Erica's wrists and punching her to the ground then pinning her hand behind her back so she couldn't get up. After a moment people around her started clapping and Aiden pushed through the crowd and looked at the girls.

"What happened here?"

Erica groaned and Juniper stood up, "She got flipped out because I bumped into her."

"What happened?" Erica said, sitting up, "How did I get here?"

"Something tells me this is the work of that girl who challenged you yesterday." said Aiden helping Erica to her feet. "Eylam take your sister to the infirmary, and uhh" he pointed at her neck.

Juniper picked up Carmine's sword and handed it back to him, "So what exactly are we supposed to do."

"We have to find her and punish her but, while it wasn't a formal challenge, you beat Erica in a fight, you are the queen of this place now."

"What?" Juniper said surprised, "It's my

second day here, isn't that fast?"

"This place is fast paced. Either get with the program and keep up or get left behind waiting for an explanation."

He grabbed her wrist and rushed down the hall into a separate room.

"Okay this you're going to explain, I didn't challenge her so I shouldn't get her rank."

"You have shown everyone that you can outmatch Erica; you demonstrated that you are more deserving of that rank whether it was a formal challenge or not."

Aiden went into a room off of the one he had taken Juniper to, and Juniper could only imagine what he was doing. After a few minutes he came back and hung a silver pendant just like the one Erica had been wearing, around Juniper's neck.

"That is the mark of the highest-ranking person, I have the matching one, the king and queen wear these always." He looked at her closely, "Don't take it off."

He pushed her out of the room and Juniper walked down the hall. As she walked, people avoided eye contact and stayed out of her way like their lives depended on it. She walked into the gym to continue working on her combat skills and saw Zane in there punching a punching bag. Juniper didn't know how to get his attention, so she looked around and saw a pad of paper with a pencil sitting on a bench, she walked over to it and wrote *'Hey it's Zane right? One of the high rankers? I'm Junie, and wanted to introduce myself,'* and walked over to him and tapped him on the shoulder. He turned around and saw Juniper standing behind him, she showed him the note pad and he started signing. Juniper wrote something else on the note pad *'I don't know sign language,'* He held up one finger and ran out of the room and came back with Aanya.

"Hello, I was told you don't know sign language."

"Yeah, I don't, by the way you're Aanya, right? We haven't formally met but Erica told me about all of you."

"Yeah, that's fine but I can translate for you."

"Thanks."

Aanya started signing while Juniper was talking and anything Zane signed, Aanya said aloud, and she joined the conversation too and they just chatted for a while. Juniper started feeling more comfortable around these people. Despite the fact that they were ranked by skill and ability to fight each other, most of the people Juniper had met had been really kind to her. After an hour or two Carmine came in, and Juniper caught his attention.

"Hey sorry about using your sword without permission earlier."

"It's fine, just give me a bit more warning next time."

"Well, I wasn't really expecting to have to fight anyone at the time."

"You're getting better with it. We might want to start thinking about getting you your own sword."

"Let's do it now then." Juniper shrugged, "It'd be helpful to spar rather than fight a training dummy."

He nodded and asked Juniper to follow him. They walked down to a forge that had a few pre-made swords on the walls.

"Am I taking one that's already made or are we making a new one?"

"We should make a new one. It's better for the wielder that way, I made the one I carry with me. You should make your own as well."

"Ok so I've never done this before."

"It's okay, I'll help you."

The next week was spent making a sword and training in combat, Juniper didn't see Erica at all during that time, but she had a nice time learning more about Carmine and got to know Circe better. The day the sword was finished, and the hilt was attached Juniper was about to unsheathe her new weapon when Aiden rushed in.

"Something's wrong, have either of you seen Eylam?"

"No Carmine and I have been in here all day."

"I thought he would be with Erica, where is she?"

Aiden shook his head, "We can't find her either, help us find them."

Juniper nodded, "Erica and Eylam are priority one, Carmine spread the word I'll search with Aiden."

Carmine nodded and Juniper ran out with Aiden to search after tying her sword to her belt. They went from room to room until the door of one room locked by itself.

"What?" Juniper yelled as she started trying to open the door.

"Oh no."

"Finally, I was starting to wonder if you'd ever notice that they were missing," said a familiar voice.

"Commander," said Aiden, turning to face where the voice, "You took the two second rankings?"

"Of course, I did, you know those two they would never just vanish."

"Commander, why have you locked Aiden and me in a room?"

"I needed you two alone together."

The Commander strolled over to Aiden and whispered something in his ear, and Aiden stumbled back and looked at Juniper with fear in his eyes. Juniper wanted to ask what the Commander had said, Aiden started shaking his head and mumbling the word no over and over again.

"So, Aiden I must ask you something, what are you willing to do for your home?"

He looked up and determination replaced fear in his gaze, "Anything."

"Then prove it."

Aiden nodded and the Commander handed him something but Juniper couldn't see what it was. Before Juniper could move Aiden attacked and she saw a glint of silver in his hand. He slashed over her; she barely managed to dodge and she felt a small cut on her cheekbone. He moved to attack again, and this time Juniper wasn't so lucky; he managed to get a decent cut on her shoulder and she felt the blood seeping down her arm. He shifted his stance and she recognized what he was going to do. Juniper had hung her new sword on her hip, now she drew it and locked its blade on the knife. She twisted it to make him lose his grip and kicked him in the diaphragm causing him to stumble back, gasping for air.

The Commander laughed, "Wow you are more powerful than I anticipated."

Juniper glared at him, "What's that supposed to mean?"

"Oh nothing, I was just trying to cause a decent distraction."

Juniper was about to ask what he meant when she felt something rake across her back. All she felt now was intense pain, she fell forward and heard something hit on the floor. Juniper managed to see what had fallen and saw a titanium blade splattered with blood. As she lost consciousness, she heard the door open and someone ran in, picked her up and began to run through the hallways.

Chapter 5

Unsure of how much time had passed Juniper managed to open her eyes. She heard people talking near her but as she tried to sit up, she felt a sharp pain in her back, and someone rushed toward her and gently pushed her back down in a lying position.

"Don't do that."

Juniper saw the person talking to her and smiled, "Erica you're ok."

"Yup I didn't take too long to recover, you didn't do a whole lot of damage."

Juniper saw a decent scar over the bridge of her nose, "Do you know what happened?"

"You mean when we fought or when Eylam found you bleeding out."

"To you."

"Okay so remember that girl who challenged you, she also has a power that controls people, I haven't figured out how it works but we obey her every order when she uses her power," Erica began, "She was mad that you beat her so she used her power on me to try and humiliate you little did she know you're a fast learner and you managed to outwit me. The scar came from when you cut me with Carmine's sword."

"I'm sorry. I didn't want to hurt you too badly." Juniper winced after she spoke.

"It's fine, scars are a common thing around here; they are normally worn like trophies."

"Erica, have you ever thought about leaving?"

"No, this is my home. I've been here as long as I can remember."

Juniper thought about her home, "So you know how important home can be?"

Erica looked confused, "Of course, we're safe here and need to protect it."

"So would you understand if I said I needed to leave?"

"Why would you ever want to leave?"

"I need to get back to my family, they must be terrified about my disappearance."

"You can't leave, you're needed here." Erica said, her voice quivering.

"I have another job for my family."

"Your family?"

Juniper looked to the side, "I need to do something important."

"How important?"

"I need you to trust me and help me escape, or

at least answer a question for me."

Erica sighed, "I'll answer your question."

"Does the Commander have powers?"

"Yes, but nobody knows what they are, there are a few theories like emotional manipulation."

After that Erica left and Juniper was alone. She couldn't sit up, so she just lay there with nothing but her thoughts to keep her company. She wondered what the Commander's powers were, or Aiden's. She was really scared of what might happen if she went back home, how her parents would react to a tattoo and the huge scar on her back. The gash on her back went from her right shoulder to her left hip from what Juniper could feel; it was pretty deep as well. Juniper knew she could heal it a little bit if she could reach it, but she was stuck lying flat on her back because it hurt too much to move. After a few minutes, someone else came in.

"Hey Junie, Erica told me you woke up."

"Oh hi, Eylam."

He smiled at her, "Does it hurt really bad?"

"It does when I move."

He laughed, "Well don't move then."

"Eylam, what are Aiden's powers?"

He rubbed the back of his neck, "He has a combination of fire powers, like pyrokinesis and pyroportation."

Juniper looked at him, "Meaning?"

"He can create, control, and teleport through fire."

"Neat, but if I'm being honest that is the most straightforward in terms of where he's from."

"What do you mean?"

"Well, of the five kingdoms he's obviously from Vulcan."

"I don't know what you're talking about."

Just then someone else came in, "Hey Eylam can I talk to you... oh."

Juniper looked over to see Aiden, "I didn't expect to see you."

"Did I miss something?" asked Eylam, confused.

"Juniper, I didn't know you woke up."

"Yeah, how long was I out?"

Aiden ruffled the hair on the back of his head, "About a week."

"Great, I've been here for two weeks and have already almost died."

Aiden looked away and seemed ashamed of his actions, "When Eylam took you here he left your sword behind I grabbed it and left it in your room."

"Thanks, I guess."

They looked away from each other unsure of what to say, "I'll just leave."

After Aiden walked out Eylam turned his attention back to Juniper, "Did something happen between you two?"

"He's the reason I'm here."

"He cut your back open, but I thought he-" Eylam cut himself off before finishing his statement.

"He what, Eylam?"

"Nothing, just forget I said anything."

Juniper wondered what Eylam was about to say about Aiden but there were bigger things on her plate right now. She figured she could heal her back, but she couldn't reach it to try. She needed to practice with them as well.

"Can you help me out with something Eylam?"

"Sure."

"I have healing powers and could try to heal my back a little bit but can't reach it."

"What do you need me to do?"

"I could reach it if I could sit up."

"Oh, I could try but it would hurt you a lot."

"I'm aware of that but I want to try anyway."

"Fine, I guess I'll help."

Eylam helped Juniper attempt to sit up and as she did a feeling of intense burning pain rushed up her spine. Juniper managed to move her hand over the bandaged wound and tried her powers.

As soon as she did the pain died down and she was able to sit up on her own.

"That looked excruciating, are you ok?"

"Much better now." Juniper sat on the edge of the bed, "Unfortunately these powers aren't so strong and this wound was too big, I did my best but this was as far as I could heal it."

"If you want to work on your healing powers you could ask the people who work in the infirmary."

"You think they'd let me?"

"Why wouldn't they? We need good healers around here."

"Sure, can you go get one of them?"

"Yeah, I'll go get Jason, he's our lead healer."

Eylam got up and left to go find Jason. As Juniper sat alone her mind wandered back to her family and what they were doing. She thought about her friends and how scared they must be, and finally, she thought about Aeolus, she was supposed to marry him but was stuck here just trying to survive.

"I'm sorry, Aeolus," she said to herself.

"Who's Aeolus?" asked Eylam as he walked in with Jason.

"Oh, um he's not important." She lied to herself trying not to get caught up in feelings.

Eylam rolled his eyes, "Anyway this is Jason he

has health-related powers."

Juniper looked at him and he started explaining to them, "I can tell how bad an injury is just by looking at it."

"Neat, I take it you don't have that high of a rank."

"Not really, my power isn't one for combat and I'm not a very physically strong person either."

"I wish I could do something, but even with the highest rank I don't think I can change yours."

"Nope I need to fight my way up the totem pole just like everyone else, I like being toward the bottom though less competition."

"I suppose being lower has its advantages, like people aren't afraid to look at you."

Jason shrugged, "I heard that you wanted to work in the infirmary, why do you?"

Juniper held out her hands palms up, "I have healing powers and want to work with them to make them stronger."

"You want to work here as training?"

"Yes, but I also want to let people know they shouldn't be afraid of me."

"That can be dangerous, if people think you're weak they'll use it to hurt you."

Eylam looked at Juniper, "He's right there's a

reason the A19902 is so cold toward everyone."

"A19902?"

"Aiden we either call him by his ID or we just call him A because he doesn't let anyone use his name."

"He lets me call him by his name."

"You were the only one stupid brave enough to do it, but that's not why he does."

"Then why does he, Eylam?"

"Moving on Jason, do you think she could work in the infirmary?"

"Quit trying to change the subject!"

"Too late Junie. Jason, answer the question."

"Of course, she can, actual healing powers would be so good in here."

Eylam nodded his head, "Cool I will leave the rest to you then, Bye!"

He walked out before Juniper could stop him, so she turned her attention back to Jason. He had a very kind smile and a calm voice. He also had golden eyes that seemed to shimmer, he had the same skin color as Erica and Eylam, but he had vitiligo, and he had black hair with patches of blond scattered around.

"Can you stand?"

"I think so."

Juniper stood up and stumbled forward a little bit, and Jason laughed, "Good you can, follow me."

He gestured over his shoulder, and she followed him into a different room with people who were hurt and sick.

"This is the main room in the infirmary. When people are in here for more than a day, we move them to our side rooms to make room for the others."

Jason gave Juniper a short tour of the infirmary and introduced her to the other healers, most of whom were nervous to be talking to her. Juniper tried her best to reassure them that she wouldn't hurt anyone and that she only wanted to help.

"Okay now that you know where everything is, and you know what to do I'll get you a list of people who don't have too serious injuries for you to heal."

Juniper smiled, "Yeah I don't think I can do anything too big, and I really don't want to risk making things worse."

"I also need to make sure that these patients consent to you using your powers on them."

"I hope that won't be an issue."

Jason smiled, "It shouldn't be, but you never know."

He walked over to a few different people and talked to them, occasionally writing things down on a clipboard. He walked back over to Juniper with a list of names.

"Wash your hands, put on some disposable gloves, and get to work!"

Juniper did as Jason instructed, and she greeted her first patient who had gotten a decent cut on her face; Juniper managed to heal it quickly and move on. Juniper went through her list faster than she originally expected and was finished before dinner. Jason smiled approvingly at her, then the dinner bell rang. All the healers got up and walked out to the cafeteria. Juniper met up with Erica and Eylam as she did every day. They walked in as Erica was telling him about what had happened in the library today and Juniper saw Aiden sitting alone as always. Juniper knew that he knew she was there, but he was desperately avoiding eye contact.

"Junie, are you listening to me?"

"What, oh um yes, sorry I got distracted."

Erica smirked, "Oh yeah, distracted looking at the hottest guy in the room."

"What no, of course not."

"Yes, you were, I think Junie might have herself a little crush."

Juniper felt her face go red, "No I don't."

"Seriously, look how much you're blushing."

"I don't like him like that!"

"You can't fool me! Eylam, back me up here."

Eylam glanced at Aiden then at Juniper, "Junie mentioned a boy named Aeolus earlier."

Erica grabbed her food and they walked to a table, "Who's Aeolus?"

Juniper sat down and glared at her, "Nobody of consequence."

Eylam placed his hands firmly on the table and stared Juniper down, "I'm good at telling when people are lying, and you my friend are lying."

Erica squinted at Juniper, "So I don't think this Aeolus is unimportant."

"Fine, he's someone I knew before I came here."

Erica slammed her hands down on her legs, "What was your relationship with him?"

Juniper rolled her eyes, "You're not going to leave me alone about this until I tell you, are you?"

"Nope, now spill."

"Aeolus was my fiancé."

Erica gasped and Eylam looked at her with wide eyes, "You were engaged as in to be married?"

"Uhh yes." Juniper shrugged, "It was arranged by our parents."

Eylam sat back, "So it was an arranged marriage, is that what I'm hearing?"

Erica who looked like she was in a daze, "Is Aeolus hot?"

"Erica!"

"What, it's a valid question."

"Eylam, what's a polite way to tell someone you want to hit them in the face with a brick?"

Eylam looked up, "One wishes to acquaint your facial features with a fundamental item used in building walls."

Erica looked impressed, "That was amazing, how did you come up with that Eylam?"

"Talent and an extensive vocabulary." Eylam replied, pushing his glasses up his nose.

"Ok but back to this boy, tell us about him, Junie."

"No, I'm not telling you about him"

As Erica demanded to know more about Aeolus, so Juniper gave her a physical description and a few things about his personality and mannerisms, she told them about the secret admirer and the shrines.

"Wow, he was really popular with the ladies."

"Very, it got really annoying for his sister."

"I'm sure it did."

They had a peaceful rest of dinner and they started walking to their rooms for the evening. Juniper walked in and saw her sword leaning against her desk, she picked it up and drew it from its sheath. Three feet of Damascus steel built into an elegant rapier, the grip comfortable and easy to hold. The sword itself was balanced and light, perfect for Juniper.

She had also become skilled in using knives and close combat. She had gotten a knife with a reverse grip that she kept strapped on the back of her belt while the sword sheath tied to the belt loops at her hip. It was a bit more difficult to use them given how tightly bandaged her torso was, however, she could still fight just as well as before.

Soon it was time for her to go to bed and she woke up the next morning feeling refreshed. Juniper went down to breakfast and saw Jason standing nervously off to the side.

"Hey Jason, are you okay?" asked Juniper.

"Yeah, just trying to get my food," he responded, looking away.

Juniper squinted at him and saw a small trail of blood trickling down his face. She followed the trail with her eyes and saw a furrow in his hair with a good-sized cut underneath it.

"You're hurt Jason!"

"No, I'm fine." He looked up and met Juniper's eyes, "Really I am."

"No, you're not, come on."

She grabbed his wrist and marched him to the infirmary, and as soon as they got there, she sat him down in a chair. Juniper touched his wound and began healing it. As soon as she was done, she pulled up another chair in front of him and sat down.

"Tell me what happened."

Jason sighed, "I had a run in with someone who woke up on the wrong side of the bed this morning."

"Who was it?"

"That's not important it's just how things go here." he paused and looked at his feet, "I was an easy target."

Juniper crossed her arms, "That doesn't make it any better. The person who did that had no real reason to lash out at you."

"I get that but-"

"No, it's just wrong and I'm going to do something about it."

Juniper got up and opened the door to see the Commander standing in the doorway, "Where do you think you're going?"

Jason got up and moved to a kneeling position while Juniper just glowered at him, "You've already tried to kill me, what do you want now."

"Oh, just for you to follow me I need to speak with you."

"How can you fathom the possibility that I would trust you enough to follow."

He grabbed the collar of her shirt and leaned down to whisper in her ear, "Because I'm giving you no choice," He let go and took a step back, "Now come along before I use my power."

She was hesitant to follow but as unaware of his power as she was, Juniper figured it was a better idea to follow. She followed him into a dark room where he seemed to have vanished. When the lights turned on, she met the Commander's eyes but he was no longer alone. He was holding Aiden and Eylam in front of him with a scheming smirk on his face.

"I know about your relationships with these two, but I need you to pick one."

Juniper looked at them, Eylam looked angry, occasionally trying to pull himself free while Aiden stood perfectly still looking at the ground in front of him.

"What do you mean pick one?" Juniper asked, her voice shaking.

The Commander raised one eyebrow still smirking, "Why, a smart girl like you should know."

Aiden looked up at Juniper and she saw panic and desperation in his eyes, and he mumbled something just loud enough for her to hear, "Pick Eylam, he doesn't deserve this."

Juniper took a couple steps back unsure of what to do. She had known what he meant and couldn't bring herself to believe him. She cared too deeply for both Aiden and Eylam. Aiden had been standoffish and mean but she could tell he had a sweet side and he was really ashamed of what he had done to her and hadn't been given a chance to truly apologize and find a way to make up for it, while Eylam had treated her like his sister. He and Erica had been so wonderfully kind to her and she couldn't pick one of them as the Commander instructed.

"Pick before I pick for you."

"I-I can't."

"Fine."

The Commander tightened his grip on the two boys, visibly startling them before pushing Aiden to the ground and in one swift movement drawing a silver knife and stabbing Eylam in the side high enough to hit a lung, before letting go of the blade leaving it in the wound and running out of the room. Aiden got to his feet and stared at Eylam in horror while Juniper rushed forward and pulled the blade from his side to try and heal it. However due to how scared she was it wasn't working.

Eylam coughed and crimson blood splattered on his lips, "Hey, stop it."

"No, I won't stop until I heal you!" Juniper said, tears streaming down her face.

"You can't, just stop and get out of here."

"I won't leave you; I can't leave you."

He grabbed Juniper's hands and smiled weakly, "Just leave, you can't heal a wound this big."

Juniper shook her head and continued trying when Erica walked in, "What's going on?"

Aiden stumbled back and Juniper ignored her to keep healing. Eylam's breathing became incredibly unsteady and weak. Erica rushed over and saw the bloody knife on the ground next to Juniper and Juniper's hands applying pressure to the wound covered in his blood. After two or three minutes Eylam stopped breathing entirely.

As tears continued streaming down Juniper's face Erica began shouting at her, "You killed my brother!!" She shouted angrily.

"No Erica, please you don't understand."

"Silence!" She used her power on Juniper, "He was the only family I had left and he's dead because of you."

Erica broke down and started sobbing, Juniper reached out and put a hand on her shoulder when Erica slapped it away and gave Juniper a death glare.

"Erica let me explain."

"I recommend you leave before I kill both of you."

Aiden reached forward, took Juniper by the

arm and pulled her away. They ran through the hallways, Aiden pulled her along into an area she had never seen before. He began to kick a panel on the wall until it came off, and Aiden started working with the things inside. As Juniper was about to ask what he was doing there was a flash of light and a doorway opened on the far wall.

Aiden got to his feel and looked at Juniper, "We can't stay here any longer, we're leaving."

Juniper was about to ask what he meant but before she could he pushed her through and they began free falling through the air.

Chapter 6

Juniper opened her eyes to see Aiden in front of her and a thick forest coming closer at an alarming speed. She managed to grab Aiden's hand and use her powers to create a cushion in the canopy. As they tumbled through the vines she made they became tangled. Juniper was stuck with her wrists bound, and some vines tangled around her torso and legs she also felt one wrapped around her throat. She looked around and saw Aiden a few feet in front of her bound in a similar way.

Aiden looked around and met her eyes, "Now what?"

"I don't know. This was your plan." Juniper replied in an annoyed tone.

"Can you use your plant powers to free us?"

"Not with the way my wrists bound, and you can't use your powers in a safe way."

"Yeah, I might live but you certainly wouldn't," He looked around, "Do you know where we are?"

"No, I only had a moment to get a hold of you

and make sure we didn't die from the fall."

After Juniper said that they heard talking, "I'm telling you I heard something crash through the canopy over here."

"Sure you did, Oliver."

"I need you to believe me, Beth."

Aiden and Juniper looked at each other and nodded, "Hey, we need help!" shouted Juniper.

"We're tangled in vines and can't get free!" followed Aiden.

The two people found them, and Juniper recognized what they were wearing; they were royal guards of Flora. When they saw Juniper, Beth dropped to a kneel and Oliver stood there with a dumbfounded look.

"P-princess Juniper."

"Please just help us down."

Beth shot to her feet, "Right away Your Highness."

The two guards helped them free, and Juniper found her sword which had fallen from her sheath and was on the ground, she still had her knife. Aiden made sure he had all his bearings and the guards led them to Juniper's palace.

They walked in and Aiden looked around warily until they came up to the doors of the throne room. As soon as Juniper and Aiden walked in, her parents turned and saw her, they stood up and pushed whatever they were doing aside like it was no longer important despite the fact that it probably was. They took a couple of gentle steps forward before they all ran and collectively hugged. When they finally pulled away, they looked at Aiden.

"Who's he?" her father started.

"Long story," replied Juniper.

Her mother was less concerned with the boy, "Where have you been?"

"Longer story."

"Whatever the story is, I'm just glad you're back safe," said her father, smiling.

Aiden took a step closer and cleared his throat, "Um hi, I'm a little confused, what's Juniper's relationship with you?"

Juniper looked at him and rolled her eyes, "Aiden, these are my parents."

"Okay, it's nice to meet you," he said awkwardly.

Her father squinted, "Charmed."

Juniper's mother put a hand on her husband's shoulder, "How do you do?"

Juniper's father told one of the servants to do something and as soon as he was given the orders the servant sped out of the room.

"Marcus what did you do?"

"I was just sending word to Aquilo that Junie

had returned dear."

The queen smiled and put her arm around Juniper, "Well then they should be arriving later today then." She looked at her daughter, "You should go get cleaned up and change."

"Of course, mom." Juniper was about to walk out when she saw Aiden still standing nervously, "Mom could you get my friend something to eat, something sweet perhaps." She said winking at him.

He smiled at her and Juniper's mother just said, "Of course, follow me."

Juniper walked to her room and as soon as she walked in, she flopped on her bed and lay there for a few minutes. She had been away from home for so long she needed a moment to appreciate the fact that she was home again. She got up off her bed and washed her face and hair then changed her clothes, being careful not to show her back or any part of her torso. She walked into the throne room and saw her parents looking over their work and saw Aiden standing in the corner looking a lot calmer than before.

Juniper walked over to him, and he started a quiet conversation, "Your mother is very kind."

"Yes, she is." Juniper looked over at her parents, "I have been told I look just like my father and act just like my mother, however, I did get my father's sense of humor."

"You really do look just like your father."

Juniper's father did have the exact same sandy blond hair, brilliant green eyes, and skin tone as Juniper, while her mother was paler, had freckles, hazel eyes, and curly black hair.

The door to the throne room opened and Juniper heard the voices that were talking hush as they saw her. She turned around and faced the royal family of Aquilo who all wore looks of surprise and curiosity.

"Junie!" Elaine shouted rushing forward to hug her friend.

Unfortunately, Aiden's fight or flight response kicked in, and in an instant, he had Juniper behind him with one hand out ready to light on fire. Elaine stopped dead in her tracks and Aeolus took an aggressive step forward.

Juniper pushed Aiden to the side, "Whoa, it's okay Aiden she a friend of mine."

Aiden took a breath and stepped back, "Sorry, I'm a little on edge."

"Sorry? You almost attacked my sister!" Aeolus growled.

"Aeolus calm down, it's how he was raised."

Aeolus looked at Aiden who glanced up, "I was told to believe everyone is an enemy."

"What does that mean?" asked Elaine, tilting

her head.

"It means I don't trust people and feel like anyone and everyone can attack me so I should always be ready for combat."

Aeolus was looking at Aiden like he was sizing him up. The visiting king and queen stepped forward causing Elaine to back up and Aeolus to back off.

"I'm sorry but who even is this boy?" Asked Aeolus's father.

"King Malachi, Queen Jacqueline, this is Aiden, a boy I met while I was missing. He helped me get back."

"Alright, but he's not going to interfere with our arrangement?" asked the king.

"No, he will not Your Majesty."

Aiden looked at Juniper, "What arrangement?"

Juniper's father looked at him strangely, "You don't know?"

"No dad he does not. He was raised very shut off from the real world, trained in combat and without even knowing about the five kingdoms."

"I can't tell if you're being serious or not."

"She's telling the truth, sir, I had no knowledge of anything happening outside my home."

"I'm sorry Aiden but you can't call it your home anymore, they'd likely kill you if you went back." murmured Juniper gently.

Aiden looked away carefully avoiding making eye contact with anyone. Juniper noticed he was pale. She looked back to Aeolus who was still watching Aiden but with more interest than aggression.

"Are you okay, Aiden?" Juniper asked, a little concerned.

"I'm fine, just tired."

Juniper looked him in the eye, "You're looking pale and weary, and you don't wear that look often."

"Well, Eylam just died, and we left because Erica was about to kill you, I think being tired is the least of our concerns."

That caught everyone's attention, "Someone was going to kill you?" asked Aeolus, his voice shaking.

"I don't think we have to worry about her, it's unlikely she'll find us."

Aiden shrugged, "The Commander could, and he might take her because she thinks we killed her brother," He looked around and his eyes fell on Juniper's collar bone, "Are you still wearing that pendant?"

Juniper's hand went to her chest where the pendant rested on its silver chain, "Yes, I am," She held up the pendant that looked like a rose, "You told me not to lose it."

Aeolus rolled his eyes, "So he gave you a gift?"

"No, I didn't." Aiden said, stepping forward revealing a similar pendant but in gold, "These are the marks of the highest-ranking. We were required to wear at all times."

As he talked, she noticed that he was getting aggravated. Aiden looked incredibly flushed. At this point, Juniper wished she had Jason's power.

"Aiden you look awful, are you sure you're feeling alright."

He faced her and she noticed his breathing had become heavy like he was trying to cool off, "I said before that I'm fine."

Juniper's father shook his head, "No you're not, you look like death." Everyone nodded their heads in agreement as her father continued, "We'll get you a room to stay in for the night but go lie down."

Juniper put a hand on his back, "You're so obviously ill Aiden, come on."

He made a noise that almost sounded like a growl before reluctantly following Juniper. He followed her to a room where a few people were cleaning. They bowed their heads and walked out. He sat down on the edge of the bed and Juniper walked over to the closet hoping there were some clothes in it. She found some that looked like they would fit and gave them to Aiden.

"Go change." Juniper instructed him.

"With you in here?"

"No, in the bathroom," replied Juniper, pointing to a door to the side.

Aiden shrugged and went into the bathroom and changed while Juniper flagged down a staff member and got a digital thermometer to check Aiden's temperature.

"What's that?"

"A thermometer, you have a fever I want to know how bad it is."

"How can you tell I have a fever?"

"Well, I doubt you're blushing because you're embarrassed though it could make sense."

Aiden felt is face and immediately looked at his hand like he was surprised, "My face is really warm."

"Yeah, that's the fever, here." Juniper said, handing him the thermometer, "put the tip under your tongue, close your mouth, and wait for it to beep. When it beeps give it to me."

He gave Juniper a weird look but did as he was told and when it beeped, he handed it to her.

"So you have a fever of one hundred and four degrees Fahrenheit."

"How bad is that?"

"It's in the typical range for the flu, but I'm

going to get our physician and-"

She was cut off by the sound of him falling backward on the bed, breathing heavily. Juniper examined Aiden as he laid there. She decided to play the role of a staff member. She adjusted him so he was sleeping with his head on the pillow and pulled the covers over his body. Juniper walked into the bathroom and got a hand towel. She turned on the faucet and soaked the towel in lukewarm water, wrang it out so it wouldn't drip and put it on Aiden's forehead.

Juniper went back to the throne room where they seemed to have just finished an intense conversation. Juniper walked silently through the room and wondered what they had been talking about.

Juniper's father cleared his throat, "So can you explain to us where you've been and how you met that boy."

Juniper didn't know how to explain where she had been and what she had seen. She shifted in place and looked at her feet.

"Junie, what's wrong?" asked Elaine

"I just can't explain it."

"Why not? It seems like it was significant because you were gone for a month," replied Aeolus a little angry.

"It's complicated. I met quite a few people, I

learned to fight and now one of the people I met wants me dead. It's not exactly easy to explain."

"Back to this girl who wants you dead, can we learn more about her?" questioned Juniper's father.

"Like I said before, it is complicated."

"You came back with two blades and a stranger, and you can't tell us about it?"

Juniper shook her head, "No I can't, I'm sorry."

Juniper wanted to tell them everything, but she believed if she did Aiden would be stuck in darkness again. He just got his freedom; she couldn't let him loose that again. She also didn't need her parents freaking out over the scar and tattoo on her back.

"Look, it's been a long day and I just got back home after a month," Juniper said, "I'm tired so if it's okay I'd like to go to my room."

Her father waved to let her know she could leave, and she made her way back to her room. She walked in and changed into something more comfortable. She put on some sweatpants and a simple long-sleeved shirt and checked her phone. When she opened up her text messages, she saw the amount her friends had texted her trying to find her. She saw all the missed calls and when she looked over at her uniform from the Facility, she saw a paper falling out of the jacket pocket. She took the paper and realized what it was. It was a request form from the infirmary she took on her first day to see if she could get it filled, it was a request from Zane asking for hearing aids with all the necessary information.

"Well, I guess he'll never get them." muttered Juniper to herself.

She guessed she could get them made. There was a knock on her door. She hid the paper in her nightstand and got up to open the door.

"Oh, hey Elaine."

"Hi, mind if we chat for a bit?"

"By all means."

Juniper stepped to the side to let Elaine in who sat down at her desk while Juniper sat on her bed.

"So, you vanish for a month, come back with a stranger who then gets sick, someone wants you dead, and you can't tell us why."

"Yes, I can't tell you where I was and what I was doing."

"So, what can you tell me?"

"Not much, other than I'm still not safe and probably won't be for a while."

"Have you contacted Victoria, Silvia, and Hazel yet?"

"No, I want to, though."

"Well." Elaine stood up and gestured to the computer, "They might be free to video chat, I'll text them."

Elaine got out her phone and Juniper got online, and Elaine sat down next to her. Soon the others came on and almost started crying.

"Junie!" Victoria shouted in excitement.

"You're okay." Silvia said immediately.

"Oh, it's good to see you again." Hazel followed.

"Calm down girls, yes I'm back and just fine."

"Where have you been?" demanded Silvia

"Long story I really can't tell."

Elaine spoke up, "She came back with a strange guy."

"Wait, what?" Hazel said in surprise, "You vanish for a month and come back with a guy?"

"Yes, I met him while I was gone, and he helped me get back."

"He didn't do anything else?" asked Victoria, "He didn't ever hurt you?"

As soon as Victoria asked that the wound on Juniper's back twinged, "No, he never hurt me."

Juniper didn't know how but Hazel saw her sword leaning on the wall in the background, "Junie is that a sword?"

"Umm, yes."

"Let us see it," begged Silvia.

"Fine, hang on."

Juniper got up and picked up her blade and drew it from its sheath and positioned it in front of the camera so her friends could get a good look at it.

"Wow, did you forge that?" asked Hazel.

"No someone I met while I was gone did and he taught me to use it."

"Another boy you met or is it the same one you brought home?" Silvia asked.

"Different boy, and no before you ask, he doesn't have a thing for me. As far as I know he was dating someone else who I also met."

"How many people did you meet."

Juniper quickly counted the people she had befriended, "I befriended eight new people, and met quite a few more most of whom were scared of me."

"Tell us their names," replied Victoria.

Juniper rolled her eyes, "The eight people I became friends with are, Erica, Eylam, Circe, Carmine, Aanya, Zane, Jason, and Aiden."

"So, who's the one you brought home and who's the one who helped you with your sword?" asked Victoria.

"Carmine is the one who made and taught me to use my sword and Aiden is the one who helped me escape." She thought about what she was saying, "If you come over, a word of warning, Aiden is a bit standoffish."

Elaine sat back, "You can say that again, he almost attacked me."

Juniper put a hand on her friend's shoulder, "His fight or flight response is going crazy because he's in such a new environment."

"Can we meet him."

"No Victoria, he came down with something on his first day of freedom and is currently resting in his room."

"I can't tell if you're being sarcastic or not."

"No, she's telling the truth. He looked like death."

The girls heard something from Hazel's line, and she had to log off.

"Sorry girls got to go, see you soon though."

"Yeah, I should go too, my brothers have been begging me to help them with their powers."

"My older sister said she was taking me ice skating today, so I have to go too."

The girls said their goodbyes and logged off. Elaine checked the time.

"Ah we're heading home now. It was good to see you home again Junie."

"I missed you all."

Elaine smiled and left while Juniper sheathed her sword and leaned it next to the bookshelf. She went over and flopped on her bed and fell asleep.

Juniper woke up the next morning feeling infinitely better, she got up and got dressed and hid a knife on her body just in case. She went down to Aiden's room to see how he was doing. He sat up when she walked in.

"Hey, feeling better?" Juniper asked.

"A little."

"Told you, you were sick."

"I know you were right. I am hungry though."

Juniper smiled, "I'll get you some food and if you're okay with it I'll use my powers to help heal your sick little self."

"Say that again and I'll burn you."

They laughed a little and Juniper left to get him some food. She walked into the kitchen and asked one of the workers to make a small meal for him. After fifteen minutes the food was ready, and she took it to him.

"Wow, I've never seen food like this," Aiden said in astonishment.

"Welcome to the life of a royal. It has perks like the best food you've ever had."

He ate the food and he looked like he had never eaten anything this delicious in his life.

"The look on your face makes it look like this is the first time you've ever eaten."

"Shut up."

"You're a sucker for good food, aren't you?"

"Fine I'll admit it." he sighed, "I'm a foodie, with a huge sweet tooth."

"I knew it, I also knew about the sweet tooth for a while."

"You did?" he looked surprised.

Juniper snickered, "Where do you think that brownie came from when I talked to you."

"I hate you."

"I know, anyway I'm going to go eat my breakfast first."

Juniper pressed her fingertips against his forehead and began using her power. She held her power for about two minutes before pulling away.

"Wow, so that's what that feels like."

"Did it feel weird?"

"A little, but you should go get your food. I'll be fine."

"See you later."

Juniper strode down to the dining hall and walked in to see her parents having a conversation. They stopped talking and turned to face her.

"How's our 'guest'?" asked her father, putting air quotes on the word guest.

"Marcus, please Juniper just got back and don't use air quotes."

"Mom, it's okay, and yes he's doing better."

Juniper's father was incredibly suspicious of Aiden, not that she could blame him. His daughter vanishes for a month then comes back with a stranger who has a big scar on his face and a resting expression that says 'try me'.

"Dad, I can tell how you feel about Aiden, but you just met him yesterday, give him a little time. This is a completely new environment for him."

"I suppose, however, he did almost hurt Princess Elaine."

"I'll have to agree with your father on that one, Junie."

"It's unlikely that will happen again, it's just how he was raised."

Her father shook his head, "You said that before, but what kind of parent raises their kid like that?"

"Aiden wasn't raised by his parents, he doesn't even know who they are, in fact nobody in that place knew who their parents were."

"Well," Juniper's mother started, "He looks familiar."

Juniper looked at her, "What do you mean?"

"Well, those red eyes, they remind me of someone."

"Now that you mention it, they do." Juniper's father replied, "But who has those eyes that we've met or know of?"

Juniper took out her phone and searched his eye color on famous people and only one person came up.

"Mom, dad, I think I found out who his mother is."

Chapter 7

As Juniper showed her parents this woman a look of terror fell over their faces.

"Wait so we don't know for sure that's his mother," Juniper said.

"Who else has that specific combination of hair and eye color?" asked her mother, "He looks just like her." Argued her mother, "Aside from the hair color."

The woman that Juniper found to possibly be Aiden's mother was the most famed assassin and criminal mastermind of the kingdom of Vulcan, Kristen Blakely, more commonly known as Rare Ruby.

"So, Aiden's mother might be a serial killer, but you can't blame someone for who their parents are right?"

"You have a point, however the most recent crime, the one that got her caught, was an assassination attempt on the royal family of Vulcan," said her father.

"Well, yeah but he can't control who his

mother is," Juniper replied.

"Fine, I'll try not to blame him for what his mother has done, but only because we don't know for sure."

Juniper's mother stepped forward, "We should find out if she is his mother."

"I'll handle that mom."

"Sure."

Juniper left and went to her room to get Zane's request form. After she got it, she went down to the physician to get something so she could find Aiden's family and see if she could get the hearing aids made. Juniper believed she would see her friends from the Facility again in the near future, and knew she could need to call a truce as they might not like her anymore. She got what she needed then headed back to Aiden's room.

"Hey, I need something from you."

Aiden was out on the balcony, "What, can I not be out here?"

Juniper rolled her eyes, "You didn't hear my question, did you?"

"No, I didn't."

"I said I need something from you."

"Oh." He walked back into the room and closed the door behind him, "What do you need?"

Juniper held a small vial out in front of her, "Some of your DNA."

"DNA?"

"Like saliva or blood."

He nodded and turned around and spat into the vial, capped it then handed it back to Juniper, "Why did you need it?" he asked, "You're not trying to clone me are you?"

"No, we're working on finding your family."

That really grabbed Aiden's attention, "You're trying to find my parents?"

"Well, we have a theory on who your mother is." She turned to leave, "I'm just hoping we're wrong."

Juniper left and took the DNA back down to the physician who gave her an idea about how long each order would take. The hearing aids were given an estimate of two or three days while the DNA results would come in about one business day. Juniper thanked him and went to the courtyard. As Juniper walked through the trees, she heard a familiar voice.

"Hmm the plants seem to be wilting more and more every day."

Juniper used her power and saw all the flowers bloom at once and heard a light gasp in surprise, "You're right. Without me here the plants seem unhappy."

"Junie? You're back?" said a girl with brown eyes and rich brown hair that was shorter than she remembered.

"Melanie, it's good to see you."

"Where have you been?" she asked excitedly.

"I've been asked that a lot."

"When did you get back?"

Juniper smiled, "Yesterday actually." Her gaze shifted to Melanie's hair, "Did you cut your hair?"

Melanie ruffled it, "Yeah, I did, do you like it?"

"Yeah, I mean I never would have thought you would get a bob but it looks great on you!"

"I hoped you would like it," she said looking away, "I actually got it cut to impress someone."

"You did?"

"Yeah, I met this guy in the castle town, we went out for dinner."

"Melanie, do you have a boyfriend?"

"Yeah, I have a boyfriend."

"That's great. Congratulations."

Melanie smiled, and met Juniper's eyes, "Thanks, but back to you, how many people know you're back?"

"Just the royal families and anyone who works in the palace."

Juniper hugged her friend and Melanie spoke, "I overheard a few maids talking about a guy who showed up yesterday, was he with you?"

"Yes, he got really sick yesterday though and he's a bit on edge so I would recommend leaving him alone for now."

Juniper heard leaves rustling behind her and she turned to see the fox pup she healed the month before pulling on the hem of her skirt.

Melanie giggled, "It looks like you've got a friend."

"Should I follow him?"

"Oh, please do."

The fox pup pulled Juniper away to some flowers it found and started rolling around in them. Juniper smiled but her happy expression quickly changed when she saw what the flowers were.

"Hey Melanie, where did these flowers come from?"

Melanie walked over and looked at them, "they showed up around the time you disappeared."

Juniper looked at them and felt their petals, "They're not poisonous."

Juniper picked one and as soon as the stem was broken a new one appeared. She had never seen anything like these before. Juniper held her hand over an open patch of dirt and tried to grow one but all that grew was a rose. The flowers themselves were roses but not natural ones. At the base of the petals, they were snow white but turned pitch black at the tip almost like they were dyed.

"It's like the Commander's hair and eyes." Juniper whispered.

"What was that Princess?"

"Oh nothing." Juniper replied

Melanie and Juniper walked back into the palace and Juniper made a mental note to ask Aiden about the flowers when she got the chance. Juniper went up to her room and put the flower in a vase. She picked one of the petals off the bud to examine it, as she looked it over the petal didn't feel dyed at all it felt completely natural. Juniper wondered about going to the library to research it, however this flower appeared when she went to the Facility so she doubted there would be anything about them. She walked over to her computer and was about to look online when there was a knock on the door.

"Come in." Juniper said, turning off her computer.

"Hey, Juniper." Aiden said, closing the door behind him.

"Oh Aiden, I thought you were resting."

He rolled his eyes, "Your healing powers work wonders on a sick person."

Juniper walked over to him, "So you would

say you're feeling normal again."

He held out his hands, "Yup."

"Good." Juniper grabbed him and flipped him over her shoulder, "And that's for almost killing me!"

Aiden didn't bother to sit up, "Yeah I deserved that."

Juniper held out her hand, "Come on get up I need to ask you something."

He took her hand and got to his feet, "What's this thing you need to ask me?"

"What can you tell me about this flower?" Asked Juniper holding out the rose for him to look at.

Aiden took the rose and examined it, "I haven't seen these since the Commander was training me."

"Wait, the Commander trained you?"

"Yeah, he basically raised me."

Juniper looked at Aiden wide eyed, "That doesn't make any sense."

Aiden looked out the window of Juniper's room and crushed the flower in his hand, "I was sold to him as a baby."

"You were?"

"Yes, the others were taken there around the age of five."

Juniper glanced around, "That's when the

royals' powers begin to develop so I suppose that makes sense."

"I was told I was showing my powers from birth, so he took me and began raising me."

"So, if kids are taken there around the age of five then wouldn't I have seen some of them?"

"No, the youngest people you encountered were sixteen, that's because before the age of fourteen they are in a different area."

"So wouldn't the youngest people I met have been fourteen?"

"No, children born with powers outside the royal families stopped appearing two years after you were born."

Juniper stepped back, "Why?"

"Not sure."

"Okay so what does this have to do with the flower?"

"He developed that flower as a way to tell people who had taken the children, the flowers were his calling card."

"But because it had been so long since he had taken someone everyone forgot what they were."

"I would assume so."

"Tell me more about being raised by the Commander."

Aiden smiled at Juniper, "Nobody has ever asked to learn about that despite the fact they all knew."

Juniper sat down on the edge of her bed and patted her hand next to her, "Well I'll be the first."

"Okay so at the age of five I began training just like everyone else, but I was alone, any other kid around that age did group training in a separate building," Aiden said, starting his story, "He started with agility and stamina, he pushed me to my limit from the start making me as powerful as he could in the shortest amount of time possible." He looked at his hands, "The course he had me run was designed for kids at the age of nine, every time I ran the course it would result in injury and pain, but I would have to get up and try again."

"That sounds rough."

"It was, by the time I was seven I managed to complete the course, he took me back to the start and said one thing, faster." Aiden looked up, "That's what he would tell me every time: 'faster'," He looked at Juniper, "When I wasn't running the course I was working with blades, hand to hand combat, and sometimes even firearms."

"And you were only seven?"

"Yes, this went on till I was ten and about a week before I turned eleven, I got the scar on my face."

"What happened?"

"I was reading a book in the corner during a meeting, he made sure I spent my off time studying. The only relaxation I got was strict sleep and mealtimes. Punishments normally meant I didn't get the privilege of food or sleep but the Commander decided that I said something so bad I deserved a bigger punishment, something I would never forget." Aiden touched the scar, his voice like broken glass.

"What did you say?"

"He was talking about a plan to take over your kingdom using flowers he made years ago as a warning that he was making an army, I asked what he meant by that, and he told me not to worry about it." Aiden clenched his fists, "He began talking about different ways to kill the royal families, as ideas were thrown around between him and the guards, I asked what they did to deserve that."

"You asked why he wanted to kill the royal families?"

"Yeah, and in response to my question he cut my face, using the same knife that he killed Eylam with. I fell backward, and he looked at me and said let that scar remind you who's in charge. you do not question my authority or orders."

"You were a young child," Juniper said.

"I know." Aiden replied, his voice breaking,

"After that, schedules became much stricter if I was one minute late to a meal I wasn't allowed to eat, if I wasn't in my room by a certain time the door would lock, and I wasn't allowed in until the next day."

Juniper hugged him, "It sounds awful."

"The worst thing was entering the main part of the Facility when I turned fourteen. I ascended the ranks as quickly as you did." He pulled the pendant out from under his shirt, "On the first day everyone saw the scar and was told that the Commander raised me personally, while I had the lowest rank because it was my first day-"

Juniper cut him off, "You didn't do that orientation fight?"

"No the Commander thought if I was powerful enough I would get to the top in a week, but even so from day one people were afraid to look me in the eye, but at dinner on the first day I had taken the first spot in line when the old king came up to me, he was about nineteen at the time, he said I was in his spot in line and told me to move." Aiden's tone changed, he sounded proud, "I told him no, if he wanted that spot, he had to get there on time, I was tall for my age and he was average I was about eye level him, he grabbed my shirt collar so I kicked him in the diaphragm."

"Wow, that seems like a bit much."

"Whatever the case he took a minute to regain his breath and he tried to strike me, but I hit him in the jaw as hard as I could knocking him out, I stepped forward and took the king pendant from around his neck and put it on saying if you lost that easily you don't deserve that rank."

"You got the highest rank on your first day?" asked Juniper, impressed.

"Yes, after that wherever I walked people scrambled out of the way, nobody dared look me in the eye let alone talk to me in fear I was in a bad mood. No one could tell what I was thinking at any given moment, after that is was just an average life, I was challenged for my rank from time to time, but the opponent always lost." Aiden rested his head in his hands, "People got badly hurt because of me."

"Aiden, you can't blame yourself for what happened to them."

"But that's just it, those injuries were my fault." She shook his head, "You were in the infirmary unconscious for a week because of me."

"No, it was the Commander. Speaking of, do you know what his powers are."

"You've been curious about them?" he asked.

"Yeah, I asked Erica, but she didn't know and only had a theory."

"I guess, I mean I lived with him for the first fourteen years of my life, and I still don't exactly know what they are."

"Do you have a general idea?"

"Yeah, I've heard some of the theories and they all revolve around the same general idea of messing with people's emotions. He can basically blackmail people into doing whatever."

"I can't help but notice a lot of people have powers relating to controlling people."

Aiden shrugged, "He doesn't control them exactly he keeps them complacent, by threatening things they care about."

"So, he keeps them broken down emotionally so he can control them when necessary."

"Basically, but I'm not entirely sure that his power or if he's just really good at manipulating people with words and threats."

When Aiden said that something in her mind clicked, "He could be keeping his real power hidden."

"What do you mean?" Aiden asked.

"He could just be gaslighting them."

"Gaslighting?"

Juniper got up and got a dictionary off her shelf and opened it and showed it to Aiden, "Gaslighting, making people question their reality or saying I know you better than you know yourself."

"Like Stockholm syndrome?"

"Exactly, he's giving them Stockholm syndrome by gaslighting them."

Then it seemed to click in Aiden's mind as well, "He's keeping his powers hidden so we can't find weaknesses?"

"Yeah, the Commander might be doing something like that."

As they continued talking about it, Juniper's father came into her room, "So what are you two talking about?"

"Oh, dad it's nothing."

A voice came from the window, "Is it now, I heard everything it doesn't seem like nothing."

Juniper stood up and faced who was speaking and froze while Aiden just glared, "How did you find us?"

The girl reached into her pocket and pulled out a small GPS, "Tracking devices."

Juniper shook her head, "Better question how and why are you here, Erica?"

Erica smiled but it was more threatening, "Aanya's power doesn't just work on herself. She can make other things exist in more than one place."

The sentence didn't seem to add up in Juniper's mind, she knew everyone's powers had limits but what were Aanya's? Juniper racked her brain to remember but the only thing she knew was what it was.

Juniper's father took a step back, "I'm sorry who are you?"

"Oh, you must be her father, I'm Erica I used to be a friend of hers before she killed my brother."

Juniper tried to step forward, but Aiden held her back, "You didn't answer the other question of why you are here."

Erica smirked, "Oh that's easy, Juniper, I know you have a theory of who Aiden's mother is and the Commander wanted me to tell you that you were right."

"Oh no."

"He's the son of a killer," she smiled sweetly, "Anyway I have other things to attend to, toodles."

Chapter 8

Erica turned and vanished out the window and Aiden was staring at Juniper, "What did she say about me?"

"She said you were the son of a killer," replied her father before Juniper could speak, "The most famed assassin in the kingdom of Vulcan."

Juniper looked at him, "Are you ok."

He reached into his back pocket and pulled out a blade, "No I'm not okay, I suppose for someone like me being the child of an assassin doesn't seem so far-fetched I mean look at you."

"What does that mean?" Juniper asked.

"You're lucky to be alive right now," He unsheathed the blade, "I used this to try and kill you."

Juniper looked at the blade and recognized it and the same one she saw clatter on the floor shortly after it raked across her back and it was still stained with her blood, "Aiden, that wasn't your fault."

"I'm sorry; he tried to kill you?" her father

said, almost yelling, "And what's this about you killing that girl's brother?"

"Dad, now's not the time."

"Uh now seems like the perfect time, not to mention we now know who his mother is."

Aiden stood up dropping the blade "I still haven't been told her name, so you know who she is, what about me?"

Juniper stepped between her father and friend, "Aiden her name is Kristen Blakely, she was an assassin known as Rare Ruby. Her last mission was to kill the royal family of Vulcan however she was caught before she could."

"How recent was that?"

"She was caught about a year before I was born."

"Considering I'm a year older that would mean I was born right before she got caught."

Juniper's father rolled his eyes, "Nobody knew she had kids or was even married."

"Well, dad she might not have been married, but now we know she has a son."

"Well, what now he's the one who allowed that girl to find us, as well as trying to kill you."

"Your Majesty, if it means anything I was being controlled."

"That doesn't help the fact that you tried to kill her, and she killed a guy."

Aiden tried to push Juniper aside and walk to her father, but Juniper stood her ground. "Juniper didn't kill him."

"Okay but who was that?"

"I mentioned the name Erica before, that was her."

"Yes, I remember you mentioning Erica, I thought I recognized the name when you addressed her."

"She's currently under the impression that Juniper killed her twin brother Eylam however that isn't true."

The king looked over Juniper and Aiden, "So why does she believe that?"

"Dad, she has real reason to believe that as when she walked in, she saw a bloody knife lying next to me and me trying to heal his wound but she took it out of context."

"Fine, I'll believe that but tell me why I shouldn't have you imprisoned for trying to kill my daughter."

Aiden looked at Juniper then to her father unsure of how to answer but Juniper knew he didn't deserve to be imprisoned, "Because I request that he be pardoned."

Aiden looked at Juniper with a look of confusion and her father gave the same look, "He tried to kill you and you want to pardon him?"

"Yes, because I already got my revenge on him."

"How exactly?"

"She judo flipped me."

He squinted at Aiden before speaking again, "Fine I'll pardon him but only because you asked." Juniper was about to thank her father, "However, he moves an inch out of line he is no longer pardoned, is that clear."

"Understood Your Majesty."

"Yes dad."

The king walked out, and Aiden looked out the window, "Why did you ask for that?"

"It wasn't your fault." Juniper replied, picking up the blade he had thrown to the floor.

"You bedridden and unconscious for a week and," he cut himself off, turning around to see her holding the blade beneath his chin.

"If I wanted you to be punished, I would have told them sooner, and if I wanted you dead you wouldn't be standing right now."

He smirked, "I suppose, now maybe I could get a short tour of your palace."

"Fine, you should know your way around as you will be living here for a while."

Juniper led him out of the room and started showing him where all the important things were. She showed him the courtyard and where the Commander's flowers were.

"So, about the flowers you know where they came from but they're impossible to get rid of."

"Good to know I'll be sure to tell the gardeners."

She then led him to the palace gym letting him know he was free to workout whenever he felt like it. He walked around looking over all the equipment and saw a few punching bags. After he finished, Juniper showed him the library.

"I've never seen so many books before."

"Are you a bookworm, Aiden?

"Not really but Eylam was. Anytime I saw him for the first couple years he always had his nose in a book."

"Is that why he wore glasses?"

"I would assume so," He looked at Juniper, "Anything else I should know about the palace?"

"Yeah, come on."

She led him to the kitchen and let all the staff know who he was, the last thing she showed him was the dining hall.

"Okay but what about the ballroom?" asked Aiden.

"The ballroom isn't important unless there's a ball."

Aiden nodded and Juniper's phone dinged, "What was that?"

"Oh, it's just my friends texting me."

"This is going to sound crazy but what's a text?"

Juniper stifled a laugh, "Right you've never left the Facility and have never seen a cellphone before."

"I have not, please help me, I get the feeling that they're a normal thing for people like us to have."

Juniper attempted to keep a straight face while explaining what a cellphone was and what it did. It was easier because he did know what a computer was, but the only ones he knew of were specialized and didn't have things like the internet. The computers at the Facility were used for studying and they weren't very good quality, so most kids stuck to book learning.

"Alright I think I get it, now what did they say?"

Juniper checked the message and sighed, "Nothing you need to be concerned about."

Aiden smirked, "Is it? Just tell me."

"It's girl stuff Aiden nothing you would even be interested in."

Juniper wasn't lying about it being girl stuff however she wasn't sure if he would be completely indifferent to it. Her friends were asking about shopping, within a second of reading that text she wasn't sure if it was safe.

"Do you know where?" asked Juniper.

"Where what?"

"The trackers, where did the Commander put them?"

"If I'm remembering correctly, it's in the tattoo."

Juniper nodded and made an attempt to remove it with her powers. She held her hand over the tattoo and felt a stabbing pain before feeling a small object in her hand. She looked at it, it was about the size of a fingernail and looked easy enough to break.

"Wow, how did you know that would work?"

Juniper shrugged, "I didn't, and it hurt I can do yours but-"

"Please, I can take pain. Look who you're talking to."

Juniper rolled her eyes then turned him around so she could reach the tattoo easier. She held her hand over the same spot and after a couple seconds his tracker broke free and was in her hand as well.

"Well, that did hurt, you were right." He stretched his shoulders, "Is it bleeding?"

"A little but you'll be fine."

Juniper took the trackers, placed them on the floor and crushed them beneath her foot.

"Well now they can't track us at all, but we should still be careful," Aiden said, looking over the destroyed trackers.

"Well yeah I figured we still weren't entirely safe."

"So, you do have other friends here."

"Yes, what about it?"

"Well, you said I wouldn't care about what you were asked to do."

"Aiden, are you asking to tag along with my friend group?"

"Just once, I want to learn more about the outside world."

"You can't come," Juniper said and Aiden looked a bit upset, "But I can find something else to do that you would be interested in."

"What kind of things are here that we can do?"

"Come on I'll show you."

She took Aiden back to her room and got on her computer to look into some fun activities to show him. As they browsed through some different things, he took an interest in horseback riding.

"Really? Horseback riding? Never would have thought you'd take an interest in that."

"How is that surprising?" He looked at Juniper.

"I mean I guess a nice ride would show you some nice things about this place and one of my friends is a dressage champion."

"Again, I'm gonna sound crazy but what's dressage?"

"A fancy style of riding, I'm sure she'd love to show you."

Aiden smiled, "Sounds like fun."

"Alright I'll text them and set it up." Juniper replied, taking out her phone.

Juniper let her friends know what Aiden asked her, and all her friends immediately wanted to hang out and meet him. Elaine asked about dress shopping and Juniper simply replied that they could go another time. Victoria said she knew a great place for a ride, and she could show them. After everyone agreed they set a time and place to meet.

Juniper put her phone away stood up and said, "We're going to meet up with them at one thirty."

"Today?"

"Yes today, also it's lunch time so if you want to eat let's go down to the dining hall."

Aiden looked confused, "The bell didn't ring," as soon as he said that he saw Juniper's face and he laughed a little bit, "There isn't one, is there?"

"Nope but if you're hungry then come on."

They walked to the dining hall and as soon as they walked in her father looked up from what he was doing and glared at Aiden before turning his attention back to his work. Juniper's mother gave them a strange look, and Aiden just looked to the side of the room nervously.

"What was that about?" asked her mother as they sat down.

Juniper looked at Aiden then to her father who mouthed the words *'Tell her,'*

Juniper sighed and thought that there was no avoiding this now, "I lied about something."

"What did you lie about?"

"I wasn't entirely fine when I came back yesterday." As she said that she became increasingly aware how tightly the bandages were wrapped around her torso.

"What do you mean?"

"I was almost killed during the month I was gone and was unconscious for a week."

Her mother was taken aback and instantly blamed Aiden, "Did you do that?"

"No, um well yes I did but-" Aiden stammered.

"While he was the one who performed the action his intent was not to kill me."

"Is there anything else you failed to mention?"

"I may or may not now have a tattoo on my

left shoulder blade."

"Wait, you got a tattoo?" her father chimed in, hearing something new.

Aiden decided to explain, "Yes but not willingly, everyone where we were had the same one, and it's not ink."

Her father looked at Juniper confused, "How can a tattoo not be ink?"

"Mom, dad don't scream but a tattoo doesn't need to be ink if it's burned into your skin."

"So, correct me if I'm wrong but you were branded?" Her mother asked, getting more and more concerned.

"Well, yes however it was used to put trackers on us to be able to find us if we left. They weren't counting on my power to summon things."

"So, the trackers aren't on you anymore?" asked her mother finally calming down.

"No. We don't have trackers on us anymore as far as I know, but that still won't make us completely safe for a while," replied Aiden.

"How long do you think you have before they decide to come after you?" asked the queen.

"As far as I'm aware they already planning to either come after us or just abandon us for the sake of their original plan."

"The Commander had no idea that I was planning an escape so it's quite possible we've managed to put a decent halt on the original plan."

"So, what was their original plan?" asked the king.

Aiden seemed to be at a loss for words, "Well, it's not important what was being planned."

"Well, if you were trying to get away from them then what they were planning must be bad," her father said, leaning forward.

Before either of them answered Juniper felt something watching her. Without thinking she put her hand on top of Aiden's head and forced it down just in time to see a knife embed itself in the table in front of him. He glanced from side to side before they heard something in the rafters.

"Juniper, look out!" Aiden shouted, running forward and knocking her to the ground.

As soon as they hit the floor there was a person in a Facility uniform clutching a sword that was stuck in the chair that Juniper was sitting in.

Juniper pushed Aiden off her and stood up, "Well did anyone ever tell you that it's rude to attempt to behead someone without their consent?"

Juniper nailed the guy who tried to kill her in the gut with her foot, which had to have drawn some blood as she was wearing heels. Juniper took the sword in her hands and using all her strength yanked it free from the chair. She was about to use it when she heard someone shout something.

"I recommend dropping that sword before someone else gets hurt."

Juniper looked up and saw the Commander holding a knife to the throat of a boy with familiar golden eyes,

"Jason!" she yelled dropping the sword, "Don't hurt him he's done nothing."

Aiden got to his feet and looked up at the Commander, "Before you do anything I must ask why you insist on using bloodshed to solve your problems?"

"I'd be careful with what you say I'm the one holding all the cards, child."

"And by that you mean you're holding a knife and are threatening the life of an innocent teenager."

He pressed the knife down on Jason's throat just enough to cause a small trickle of blood and Jason started shaking a little.

"Don't hurt Jason, he's always been loyal to you, hasn't he?" Juniper said.

"So was Aiden before you came along, Princess. You changed something in him."

"What do you want?" Aiden growled, "You wouldn't be here if you didn't want something, and you obviously want us alive or you wouldn't have been so sloppy in the murder attempts."

Jason looked down at them with pure fear in his eyes before the knife moved again and he took a small step back.

"Now, now, Aiden no need to get aggravated you know why I'm here. I want to make a deal."

"Let Jason go then we'll talk," Aiden said, his tone calm and steady.

The Commander smirked, "I wouldn't have him here if he wasn't my bargaining chip."

Juniper took a step forward and placed her hands on the table, "What are you asking for?"

"Well Princess whether you believe me or not I'm not head hunting you; while you joining my side would have been nice I doubt I could convince you to join me. No, I want Aiden back on my side."

"So, what are you asking from me."

"Easy. I will free Jason from my containment and in return Aiden comes back to the Facility with me."

"You seriously expect him to accept those terms after everything you've done to him."

"Juniper he'll kill Jason if I don't accept, you know that. The Commander will stop at nothing to get what he wants."

"Aiden, you can't, we'll make a different offer."

Aiden looked sad, "You know we can't do that,

I'm sorry Juniper." Aiden turned his attention back to the Commander, "You've got a deal. You let Jason go and I go back with you."

"Look at you, sacrificing yourself for others. When did you get a heart? I thought you lost your moral code."

"There's just one thing I have to do first."

"Fine go on."

Aiden turned toward Juniper and hugged her; Juniper didn't know how to react. She just started crying.

Aiden pulled back and looked her in the eyes before kissing her gently on the cheek, "Don't cry, you'll stop him I promise."

They hugged one more time before he walked away. The Commander sheathed his knife and shoved Jason to the floor in front of Juniper. Jason sat on his knees holding his throat, shaking.

"That's an obedient warrior."

"I'm not a dog, don't talk to me like I am one."

"You're right." The Commander grabbed Aiden's upper arm, "You're a weapon, you can use a spear as a walking stick but that doesn't change its nature."

The Commander reached into his pocket and pulled out a small device and pushed a button on it and Jason cried out in alarm. "His tracker has been deactivated. I'll leave you be for now."

The Commander pushed a different button and he vanished with Aiden, and the other warrior that was with them leaving Juniper, Jason and her family stunned and scared.

"Jason are you-" Juniper started to ask.

"Do I look okay?" Jason shouted, cutting Juniper off.

"Jason let me see your throat."

"Why, so you can kill me?"

Juniper was taken aback by that comment, "Jason you need to take a few deep breaths and clear your head so you can think rationally."

"I'm sorry Juniper it's just with all of a sudden being thrown into a new place that is so much brighter, wow I'm being blinded."

Her parents gave him a strange look and she glanced over to them, "There was very little natural light in the Facility it was well lit but somehow still dark."

"Okay. Junie sorry for lashing out, can you?" He shifted his gaze down then back up to her eyes quickly.

"Yeah, I can." She said, reaching out gently, touching the incredibly small cut on his neck.

"Thanks." He said as Juniper healed his cut and helped him to his feet.

"I suppose since it's already prepared you can stay in Aiden's room."

"Alright, back up who is he and why should we trust him?" Juniper's father asked.

"Dad, Jason saved my life, he was the head healer and is the one who treated my wound when Aiden almost killed me."

"I wouldn't have managed to if Eylam hadn't found her and brought her to me," He paused before coming to a realization, "Eylam, Erica told everyone you killed him and betrayed everyone. Please tell me that's not true."

"It's not true. The Commander killed Eylam, Erica just took what she saw out of context."

"Okay, good that just seemed off."

"Jason, you do understand that you are free right you don't have to be nervous to look people in the eye, right?"

"Why do you ask."

"You still seem wary about making eye contact with me."

"Junie are you alright?"

"I'm fine, I just need a minute." Juniper looked around and saw the knife still stuck in the table and the sword that had been left on the floor.

"Junie, you don't look okay," her mother said gently.

Juniper sighed, "I'll be right back."

Juniper turned and left the room before

anyone could say a word. She sped down the halls, her arms felt numb and heavy. She got to her room and closed the door behind herself, as soon as the door clicked, she broke down. Juniper fell to her knees crying. She had lost two friends to the Commander, and she was lost. Juniper looked at her bed and saw Aiden's knife still laying there. Juniper got up and sat on the edge of her bed and held the knife in lap.

"I'm sorry I failed to save you too, Aiden." Juniper said before starting to cry again.

Chapter 9

Juniper was awoken by the sound of a thunderstorm raging outside. She got up and walked toward her balcony doors to get a better look at the storm and caught a glimpse of herself in the mirror. She had awful bedhead and her makeup was smeared all over her face from crying. She had also fallen asleep wearing her dress from yesterday.

Juniper walked into her bathroom to wash her face and change. After about half an hour she walked back out to the bathroom wearing something a bit more comfortable with her hair down and all her makeup washed off. She walked back and sat down on the edge of her bed when her phone dinged. She checked it and saw several dozen missed calls. She was about to check who called her, but her phone started ringing before she could.

"Hello?"

The voice on the other line came on, "Junie what happened to you yesterday?"

"Oh Silvia, what are you talking about?"

"Yesterday we were going to go horseback riding. You set it up and bailed with no warning."

Juniper thought for a moment before it clicked, "Ah sorry Silvia something happened, and I couldn't make it."

"Well, a phone call would have been nice, we tried calling you but you didn't pick up." Silvia said, a little annoyed.

"Look Silvia I really don't want to talk about it, so I'm gonna hang up and end the conversation here before you find some elaborate way to trick me into telling you."

"But Junie-"

Juniper cut her off by hanging up. She looked back to her balcony door to see the rain pounding against it.

"Well, the weather matches my mood." Juniper said to herself.

She contemplated sitting alone in her room all day but then figured Jason needed help so instead, she walked down the hall to the room she'd said he could use and knocked on the door. She heard footsteps and Jason opened the door to greet her.

"Junie, didn't think you would even leave your room today."

"Yeah, I just need to talk to someone who can

understand what happened."

Jason stepped out of the way and Juniper stepped inside. Before she could say anything there was a loud clap of thunder right outside the windows of the room. Jason yelped, startled by the sudden noise.

Juniper laughed a little, "This is really new to you."

"It's a flash of light followed by an incredibly loud noise. How are you not spooked by that?" Jason asked, annoyed by Juniper's teasing.

"Believe it or not but thunderstorms are normal." Juniper said patting Jason on the head, "you get used to it, it can still spook you if it's really big but for the most part it doesn't bother you."

Jason pushed Juniper's hand away, "If you say so, but are you okay?"

"I'm not sure, I mean physically I'm not hurt but I'm pretty torn up about Aiden going back."

"He risked so much to leave only to go right back to the very place he'd finally escaped for me..." Jason paused and looked away from Juniper, "I-is this my fault?"

"No, Jason, don't blame yourself for that."

"But if I had been stronger, then I could have done something."

"Jason, the Commander had a knife to your

throat threatening your life there was nothing you could do, don't blame yourself," Juniper said reassuringly.

Jason looked like he was on the verge of tears and Juniper didn't know what to say to change his mind about how he felt. She didn't say anything, instead she wrapped her arms around him. All the tension in his shoulders slipped away and he just let her comfort him.

"So," Jason said, calmer now, "This is the real world."

"Yeah, welcome to my home, Flora." Juniper replied.

Then Juniper's mother walked by, "Hey we've got planning to do and we're heading over to Aquilo, get ready."

"You're leaving?" Jason said, "In that!?"

"It's called an umbrella, Jason." Juniper turned around and faced her mother, "We might need to bring him. I get the feeling he'd have a mental breakdown in the first fifteen minutes of being alone."

Juniper's mother looked Jason up and down, "I suppose, but he'll have to change."

"I'm sorry what's wrong with what I'm wearing?"

Juniper put a hand on his shoulder, "You're still wearing the Facility uniform, I'll call someone to help you find something more appropriate for the occasion."

Juniper walked back to her room and caught one of the servants and asked him politely to help Jason. Juniper changed into something better suited to leaving her palace, clipped her hair out of her face neatly but left it down, and did some simple quick makeup. Juniper was about to head down to leave but got the urge that she was forgetting something. Juniper looked at her computer desk and saw her knife laying there, Juniper thought about leaving it but grabbed it and tucked it away in the folds of her dress.

As Juniper walked into the entry hall she saw her father questioning Jason, "So is your hair naturally blond like that or..."

Jason shrugged, "Been like that all my life, vitiligo does the same thing to my hair-" Jason held out his hands, "-that it does to my skin."

"I think it looks nice," Alice said.

"Two years of the other healers saying that and calling me pretty boy," Jason said, "It starts to lose meaning."

Juniper walked up to his side, "Why were they saying that to you for two years?"

Jason buried his hands in his pockets, "I had a crush on someone and was too cowardly to ask them out, they kept saying it to 'boost my confidence', but what's the point when you're bottom of the totem pole and your crush isn't?"

"You had a crush on this person for two years and never asked them out?" Juniper asked.

"Yeah, shut up, so anyway where are we going again?"

The king was signing something as he answered, "The neighboring kingdom."

"So, there's more than one?"

"Jason, there are five kingdoms." Juniper said.

Jason shrugged and the group walked outside to the car. As they drove through the streets, Jason looked around awestruck by everything he saw. Juniper watched as he looked at everything and couldn't help but smile. With what happened yesterday this helped a little.

They arrived at the palace and Juniper almost forgot how gorgeous it was. The Flora palace seemed to be a whole ecosystem, while the palace of Aquilo seemed to be steeped in clouds. It had snow-white walls with light blue roofs. It had plenty of windows and had an open-air style of architecture. They walked inside as the rain was stopping. As they entered the great hall they were greeted by Elaine and Aeolus who seemed to be teasing each other.

Jason leaned down and whispered to Juniper, "Who are they?"

"Prince Aeolus and Princess Elaine."

"Elaborate on why we're visiting them?"

"That is my betrothed and his sister, we're planning a wedding."

Aeolus started walking forward, cutting off Elaine's sentence to greet them, "Hello Your Majesties and Your Highness, how do you do?"

Juniper was about to answer when one of the staff members tripped and landed on her foot strangely. She winced as she tried to get up, Juniper was about to check on her when Jason put his hand in front of her and walked to the staff member instead. As he walked closer his eyes started glowing, he knelt next to her and looked at her ankle calmly.

He held out his hand and helped her up, "All it needs is some ice."

Elaine stepped forward "What did he just do?"

Juniper didn't answer instead she whispered to herself, "So that's what his powers look like, his eyes light up."

"What, Junie, do you know what he just did?" Elaine asked.

Juniper looked at her friend, "Yes, I do."

Jason walked back over, "Why are you all looking at me like that?"

"Jason," Juniper said, "What exactly do you

see when using your power?"

"It's a little complicated and takes a bit of focus but if the person isn't hurt or sick then I see a rundown of a basic physical, like breathing, heart rate, blood pressure, reflexes, and things like that."

Juniper nodded, "And if they're hurt or sick?"

"If they're sick then I can see symptoms even if they haven't shown themselves. I can see how long the virus or toxin has been in their system, and how long till they recover, if they can without treatment." He paused, "I had to manually learn what to do in case of illness my power won't tell me. It's the same with injuries."

"If someone has a disease and didn't know, would you know?"

"Actually yes."

"Now if someone is hurt what do you see then?"

"If the injury isn't a wound then I can see the damaged area and have a general idea of how it might have been hurt, I can also see how long the injury has been there," Jason thought for a moment, "If it's a bleeding wound then I see vitals, I know how much blood they have already lost and how much they're losing per second, I can tell how deep it is, angle of entry, and if I can save them."

"Okay I'm confused, you have powers despite the fact I've never seen you before." Aeolus said.

Jason looked confused, "Um, I'm not from around here."

"Okay, Elaine remember those names I listed as people I met while missing."

"Yeah, I remember, Junie, why?"

"Can you list those names for me again?"

"Umm, sure if I remember correctly, they were, Erica, Ethan, Circe, Carmine, Aanya, Zane, Jack, and Aiden."

"Close. You got two names wrong."

"How close was I to the right name?"

The names were Erica, Eylam, Circe, Carmine, Aanya, Zane, Jason, and Aiden."

"Ah, I was close."

"Anyway, this is Jason, he actually saved my life."

"He did?" Aeolus said, a bit surprised, "What happened to the other guy?"

"Aiden? Um, something came up and he had to leave."

Aeolus nodded, "So Aiden the one you initially came back with has to leave and this guy shows up and we just have to go with it." Aeolus paused before gesturing to him, "He even has powers."

When Aeolus gestured to him Jason flinched

like he thought Aeolus was going to strike him, "Aeolus listen, Aiden had powers too. It turns out that powers aren't exactly impossible to have among the townsfolk."

"What's that supposed to mean?" Elaine asked.

"Remember I was gone for a month, and I met a lot of people all of whom had powers."

Aeolus held up a hand, "Like what kind of powers?"

Juniper gestured toward Jason who flinched again, "He just explained his."

"I'm sorry to cut in but when both of you made a gesture to him, he flinched," said Juniper's mother.

"Jason, are you okay? You know nobody is going to hurt you right?"

"I know but I can't help it, being the bottom of the totem pole for five years and kinda being a punching bag for people in bad moods makes you really paranoid that someone is going to hit you."

After hearing that the group seemed at a loss for words. Aeolus looked over Jason and realized how nervous he was. Juniper noticed as well and made eye contact with Aeolus, and they exchanged a silent conversation.

Aeolus cleared his throat "Well you must be

hungry; it is around noon so would anyone like some lunch?"

"Lunch sounds great, Aeolus, follow me," Elaine said with a smile.

Everyone walked down the halls of the palace to the dining hall. As they walked Juniper watched the way Aeolus and Elaine kept looking at each other; they seemed to be having a silent conversation.

The group walked into the dining hall and sat down at the table, "Our parents will be joining us in a few minutes." Aeolus said, sitting down next to his sister.

"Juniper, your friend does know basic table manners, right?" asked her mother.

"I don't know Jason, do you know your table manners?" Juniper asked, hoping he would say yes.

"No, the cafeteria at the Facility had no actual rules, just a few unspoken rules like don't steal or ruin other people's food."

Elaine looked at him strangely then looked at Juniper, "Junie you spent a month living there with people who would ruin meals."

"Well, fights would break out in the hallways but strangely enough not a single fight broke out during a mealtime. It was honestly surprising."

Jason tapped his fingers on the table, "Aiden

made sure no fights broke out, any time one did someone would be in the infirmary with second to third-degree burns and a couple of broken bones."

Aeolus was taken aback, "Pardon?"

"Fights stopped happening after maybe three occurrences after I showed up and I can only imagine what it was like before."

"Wait just a minute, second to third-degree burns and broken bones, what did he do to them?" Aeolus asked.

Jason looked Aeolus dead in the eyes and spoke quietly, "Never make Aiden mad if you value your life, he doesn't take disrespect lightly."

The next few minutes were quiet, nobody knew how to respond to what Jason had said. The knife Juniper had taken with her felt heavy in her pocket and her back wound twinged. It had closed but she kept the bandages on not wanting to make it worse. Aeolus was looking at his sister and their silent conversation started again. If Juniper's parents were startled by what was said they didn't show it. Luckily for the group, all the tension was broken when King Malachi and Queen Jacqueline entered.

"Good afternoon everyone is feeling well I hope," said the king, unaware of the amount of tension in the room.

A small conversation was started between the royals and Juniper whispered something to Jason, "Tip number one don't rest your elbows on the table, it's bad manners."

"Thanks for the tip before I made that mistake," replied Jason, "But is there anything else I should know?"

"Don't slouch, never talk with your mouth full, don't gesture with utensils in your hands, refrain from criticizing the food, chew with your mouth closed, and wait until everyone is served before eating."

"Are you sure that's all? I don't want to embarrass you or myself."

"There are a lot of different utensils so when in doubt look at the utensil I'm using." Juniper offered.

"So, Juniper, you've brought a friend?" Queen Jacqueline asked.

Jason looked down not wanting to say anything wrong and Juniper nodded, "Well yes, it's a long story."

Jason started drumming his fingers on his leg, getting uncomfortable being around all the strangers. Juniper wondered how she could make him more relaxed, but nothing came to mind. Juniper glanced over to Elaine who subtly shrugged and shook her head.

"What happened to the other guy, the one who we met when you came back?" Queen Jacqueline continued, "Did he leave or did more people come back with you than we originally knew?"

Juniper was startled by that question as she was hoping to avoid talking about Aiden, but she knew there was no avoiding this question, "Yes, he left but his leaving resulted in Jason getting left here."

"So had Aiden not left this boy would not be here?" The king questioned.

Jason noticed that Juniper was getting upset having to talk about this so he stepped in, "Yes, if Aiden hadn't left, I wouldn't be here. In fact I wouldn't be alive."

"What exactly do you mean by that?" asked Elaine, curious about the full story.

"Well, the man that Aiden went back with was holding a knife to my throat and said he would let me go if Aiden left with him. By Aiden going back to the very place he had been trying to escape he saved my life."

"That sounds really noble actually," Aeolus said, a little impressed.

"But speaking of those two, they lived away from the five kingdoms their entire lives. We did learn who Aiden's mother is but what about your family, Jason?" Juniper's father asked.

Jason froze at that question, he like everyone else was taken at the age of five so Juniper had assumed he didn't remember his family. However now Jason seemed scared to answer the question.

"Um w-well, I don't really know." Jason said, stumbling with his words, "I have a father."

"What?" Asked Juniper, "Did you just say you have a father?"

Jason stared down not looking at anyone as their food was brought out, he took a deep breath and looked at Juniper, "Yes, unlike most others I remember my father, I didn't talk about it because I didn't want to give more ammunition to the people who would actively fight me."

"Jason if you remember his name or anything about him, we could find him."

"Yeah but, I remember everything I knew about him, and I was the only family he had." Jason said looking away, "What if he doesn't want to meet me, what if he hates me because I left him alone for fourteen years."

"I doubt that's true, I'm sure he'd love to see you."

"What if he has a new family, there are so many things I don't know."

"Jason, calm down if you're okay with it. I'd love to help you find your father."

"Okay, but let's do that later."

Chapter 10

Lunch went by without much conversation. Most were unsure how to respond to a conversation about a family member one hasn't seen in so long. After lunch, the staff cleared the table and brought some plans and papers for the group to look over.

"Now that that's out of the way, we have work to do," said Malachi.

"Work?" asked Jason.

"Right, the only ones I told before leaving were Erica and Eylam."

"But what kind of work?"

The others looked at Jason, "Why do I get so many blank stares when I ask a question?"

"Well, it's a question we don't expect people to ask," started Aeolus, "It's common knowledge for people."

"Jason more specifically it's known by people who aren't-" Juniper finished by gently tapping his facility tattoo.

"I'm sorry Junie, what was that little tap on

his shoulder?" asked Elaine.

"It made sense to me, but my question still wasn't answered."

Marcus sighed, "We're planning a wedding."

"Ah okay you did mention that earlier, I won't say anything else."

"Anyway, that seems like the biggest thing," continued Marcus.

Aeolus nodded, "Considering everything that's been happening lately we might want to hold it soon."

"Actually, I was thinking the opposite." Juniper replied.

"If it's alright for me to ask, why?" Queen Jacqueline asked.

"Well, as previously stated with everything that's been happening it would really be a safer option to wait."

"How exactly would it be safer?" Aeolus asked.

"How should I put this?" Juniper started, "I did mention a girl who was angry with me, and a few friends who are more likely going to side with her considering that they've known her longer."

Jason nodded in agreement, "They're strong. Not even Aiden could take them all on at once. Sure he could hold his own, but he would exhaust himself before he could beat them all so chances are you wouldn't do much better."

"What I'm hearing is if they were to show up it would result in a fight," said Elaine.

"That's exactly what would happen," Jason replied.

Before anyone could reply there was a scream outside one of the windows and when they all turned, they saw a short girl dangling from the wall holding on for dear life. She had long black hair and a gun in a holster on her side.

"Aeolus, do those windows open?" Juniper asked, starting to panic.

"Uh yeah but-" He started replying.

"The outside is still slick from the rain she'll fall and it's too far from the ground it's unlikely she'll survive it," Juniper said to herself, rushing to the window.

Juniper used her powers to elevate herself so she could reach the girl. Juniper reached forward and pulled the window open and held out her hand for the girl to take. The girl's hand was slipping. She looked around and made eye contact with Juniper who got a good look at her face.

"Junie!"

"Take my hand before you fall!"

She took Juniper's hand right as her hand slipped from its hold. As she fell, she almost took

Juniper with her, but Juniper had a sturdy vine wrapped around her. Juniper housed the girl on the windowsill, and she immediately threw her arms around Juniper.

"We were so worried about you after you left two days ago, we all started searching and then-" The girl started ranting.

"Hey, hey, hey," Juniper said, getting her to calm down.

As Juniper looked her over, she noticed a few scars lacing her arms and legs. Her grape purple eyes glistened with adrenaline and joy.

"Aanya, it's nice to see you but how did you get here?"

"Well Carmine overheard a conversation between the Commander and Aiden, and he found out how you left, and he told the rest of us and-" She paused and looked around, "Where are the others?" She shouted, alarmed.

"Aanya, first lower your voice, and others who came with you?"

"Carmine, Circe, and Zane," replied Aanya.

Juniper thought for a moment: when she and Aiden had left, they appeared in Flora together so why hadn't the others?

"Erica didn't go with you?" Juniper asked, hoping she'd say no.

"No, she didn't. She seems angry and a bit

unstable since Eylam died. She said you killed him."

"And you don't believe her, despite the fact you've known her longer than me?"

"Of course not, I haven't known you for a long time, but I know enough to believe you would never take a person's life."

"Good, anyway, why are you here?"

"Well, we wanted to find you because we got really worried. You almost died, then Eylam dies, then you and the king vanish, and it all happened in such a short amount of time."

"So, what was your plan for when you found me?" asked Juniper.

Aanya paused like she wasn't expecting that question, "To take you back, unless your rank is taken by challenge we're stuck without a queen, and Zane is the prince now but we're going to be in deep trouble if we don't get back soon."

Juniper debated whether to tell her she couldn't go back, then decided not to and offered something to stall her long enough to figure out a way to make the group stay.

"Before we go, we should find Circe, Carmine, and Zane."

"Yeah, but how do we find them?"

"Well, this is going to be frustrating."

Aanya faced the rest of the group Juniper was

with and Juniper discreetly used her powers to remove Aanya's tracker.

As soon as Juniper felt the tracker in her hand, Aanya yelped, "What was that?"

"I don't know." Juniper replied innocently.

Juniper crushed the tracker and helped Aanya to the floor. The royals looked at Aanya with the same look they had when meeting Aiden and Jason, except for one person at the table.

"You know I should be surprised about her showing up out of nowhere but at this point, it's far from the strangest thing to happen this week," Jason said with an exasperated sigh.

Aanya gave Jason a questioning look, "Do I know you? You seem familiar."

"Yup, leave it up to the high rankers to forget the bottom of the totem pole." Jason said to himself, but it was clear he wasn't trying to hide it.

"Wait I recognize you now. Eylam talked about you and so did Erica, you're the..." Aanya paused trying to find the right word, "Oh the gay one, right?"

Jason's face dropped into his hands, and he looked like he wanted to die, "No," he said quietly.

"Oh, it's not you, I could have sworn that Eylam liked one of the healers."

"H-he did?" Jason asked, his voice breaking a little.

"Oh, sure he could have sworn it was you, he said it was the one with black and blond hair and golden eyes."

Jason was taken aback by that statement. Juniper couldn't tell if he was happy or disappointed, they made eye contact and he quickly looked down.

"Of course, we liked each other, and I never managed to man up and ask him out I was too worried he wouldn't like me." He shook his head, "Well it's too late now, no matter how much I might want to I can't go back in time."

"Did I say something wrong?" Aanya asked.

Juniper shook her head, "No, we just didn't know that Jason was gay, I'm not sure he wanted anyone to know."

Aanya nodded, as well-intentioned as she was, she was a bit of an airhead. She, like Elaine, wasn't the best at keeping secrets; all she wanted was to make others happy. She was also ridiculously powerful. She may have been four foot ten, but nobody dared anger her for fear of their lives.

"So, there's still more of you showing up and hanging out acting out of turn around you." said Marcus.

"I'm sorry, how exactly am I acting out of

turn? She's my friend."

"Aanya please be a bit more polite," Juniper whispered.

Aanya gave her an annoyed look before asking, "Why?"

"That's my father, please have some respect." Juniper said, keeping her tone low and calm.

Aanya rolled her eyes and checked her pistols. There were two pistols held in a shoulder holster under her jacket and the other was in a holster on her thigh that looped around her leg and attached to her belt with pouches on her other leg filled with ammunition and first aid supplies. Her hair was in a side braid and her uniform was a pair of shorts, combat boots, the regular white t-shirt tucked in and the black jacket, a different variation of the same uniform all the Facility members wore.

"I'm sorry, is she carrying a couple of guns?" asked Malachi with an alarmed tone.

"Yes, I carry two guns they're not twin pistols, but I can thread a needle with these bullets."

By the way, Aanya was talking. It was clear the royals had offended her, but she was trying to keep her temper under control. Aanya knew she had a temper but because Juniper asked her to be respectful, she didn't let herself explode. Juniper wondered if the fact she had been separated from

Zane, Circe, and Carmine was a factor in her anger.

"So, this is also one of your friends, and she carries two guns?" asked Alice, "Does she have a license for those?"

"I'm trained to use these. It was my primary training after judo," replied Aanya, finishing securing her holsters.

"Being trained and being licensed aren't the same thing," Jacqueline said.

Juniper leaned down to whisper something in Aanya's ear, "I'll help you get licensed but first we should find the others."

Aanya nodded and started looking around the room with confusion in her eyes, "So now that we've finished that discussion where am I?"

Jason stood up and faced her, "The real world, where would have grown up if we hadn't been born with powers."

"Are powers not a normal thing."

Aeolus scoffed, "Uh no."

Juniper looked at Aanya, "Out of everyone in this room two don't have powers and three have powers that they shouldn't have."

"Three?" Elaine said.

"Me, I have powers I shouldn't have you know this."

"Jason and I aren't supposed to have powers

either so we were taken somewhere else where we could train them safely." Aanya stated, "That makes much more sense now."

"The reason nobody knows is because nobody could find the missing kids."

"So, what would happen if word got out that we had powers that are possibly dangerous?" Aanya asked.

"Possibly dangerous?" said Marcus, "What kind of powers do you have?"

Aanya looked to Juniper, "Can I show them?"

Juniper waved her hand in front of herself and took a step back while Aanya stepped forward. Aanya closed her eyes and appeared behind the other royals.

"Hello," said the copy.

Everyone at the table jumped and turned around. They took a minute looking from the real Aanya to the fake one. After a minute the copy disappeared, and everyone looked at Aanya wide-eyed.

"It's called omnipresence I can exist in several places at once, but I only have a five-hundred-foot radius."

Juniper's mind went to her encounter with Erica from the day before and she had to ask, "Does your power work on things that aren't you?"

"No, I can only project myself as I am."

"Erica lied to me; I could have gotten her out of there," Juniper said to herself.

Jason paused, "What's this about Erica lying to you?"

"Ah, never mind it's not important."

Juniper's phone pinged and Juniper got it out to check. When she checked the notification, she saw a familiar face had gotten arrested in Vulcan.

"Aanya back to your question about what would happen if word got out about your powers, I have an answer."

"Circe got arrested?" Jason said, "What does that even mean?"

"You get detained by authorities for breaking rules to put it in simple terms." Aeolus replied.

"Why did she get arrested?" Aanya asked, "Does that thing say."

"First, it's called a cellphone, I'm going to need to teach you about this later," Juniper started, "Secondly no it doesn't say why, all it says is a girl matching the physical description of Circe got arrested in the first precinct in the Vulcan castle town."

"They had to have had a reason for arresting her, they can't just do that for no reason she had to have done something," said Alice.

"Circe isn't a violent person by nature, right?"

Juniper said to Aanya.

"Yeah, in the years I've known her she's never attacked anyone without a reason. If she did attack someone, she must have felt threatened," replied Aanya nodding her head, "Circe would never start a fight herself."

"It can't be that hard to make Circe feel threatened," said Jason, crossing his arms.

Juniper looked at him, "How do you figure that?"

"Well, birds can be..." Jason paused for dramatic effect, "Jumpy." he finished with a smirk.

Aanya started laughing, and Juniper shook her head trying to hide the smile on her face. The others didn't get the joke and couldn't understand why Aanya and Juniper started cracking up.

"Say that to her face I dare you," Juniper said.

"Yeah, no thanks I choose life," Jason replied.

"Anyway, next available opportunity we need to go get her."

"Why exactly, she should be fine," said Marcus, rather annoyed about how events were unfolding.

"Dad, she's in danger we need to find her before someone else does."

"Who's after her?" asked Aeolus, "And why? You're not being very descriptive."

"The same person who took me is after her and considering how they've broken the rules just to be here, I'd say there's a fair chance he won't take rule-breaking like this lightly." Juniper said in a threatening tone.

"Okay, but why does this strange guy want her?" asked Aeolus, still wanting to know more.

"Her powers. She's a shapeshifter, the people who ended up here are the highest-ranking from where they came from," Juniper said, "They are immensely powerful, and useful assets to the game he seems to be playing with us."

"What do you mean game?" asked Elaine.

Aanya was about to say something, but Juniper held up a hand in front of her to keep her quiet, "I've said this once I'll say it again," Juniper started, "It's complicated, and difficult to explain."

The group wanted to ask more questions but knew Juniper wouldn't answer them. Juniper got out her phone and started searching for other people showing up around the five kingdoms. As she searched, she found an article that went up around the same time Circe's did. A stranger fell through the roof of a well-known couple from Terra.: a musician named James Mousai and his wife Ava Mousai a well-known author.

The attention this one had been getting was due to the fact that the teenage boy that crashed through their roof was taken to the hospital and looked vaguely like the couple. The description of the boy who was taken by the ambulance matched Carmine almost exactly.

"I found Carmine too," Juniper said showing the screen to Aanya and Jason "And he's in worse condition than Circe."

"Well, who do we go after first?" Jason asked.

"I'd say Carmine, for a few reasons, one he's closer and two Circe can hold her own in a fight, Carmine is hurt and needs my healing powers."

Carmine was closer location wise to the group. The five kingdoms had borders that made a pentagonal shape. From where they currently were Terra was the next kingdom over with Flora on the other side. The way the kingdoms were laid out there was a huge area of land left untouched by the kingdoms, it wasn't big enough for its own kingdom so the five royal families established a shared city called Providence. It was occupied by people of all kingdoms. Vulcan was on the other side of Flora with Oxidane found between Vulcan and Terra. Due to this layout, Vulcan where Circe was, was on the other side of Providence from Aquilo.

"When do you think you need to be there?" Asked Malachi.

"Well, people's lives are at stake so this fairly

important and I need to get there soon."

"But, how do you know he'd get killed if whoever it is your talking about found him first?" asked Elaine

"Because he's done it before. He was also about to kill Jason yesterday."

"So, this is the same guy?" Marcus asked.

"Yes, it is," Juniper replied.

Marcus turned away from his daughter. He twisted his wedding ring, something he often did when making a hard choice or if he was nervous. This was mostly because his wife was smart and even with her right next to him, he couldn't always ask her opinion so his hands went to his ring a reminder she was there even if she wasn't. Juniper always found it sweet, but she knew he was embarrassed by his habits. He glanced over to his wife, and she shrugged.

Marcus sighed, "You're right, and you know way more about the situation I'll trust you to handle it how you see fit."

"Thank you, dad," Juniper said.

Before anyone could say anything, Juniper grabbed Aanya and Jason by their wrists and dragged them out of the room with her. She walked through the hallways back to the great hall and took them to the car. She told the driver where to go and they left to go find Carmine.

Chapter 11

They were driving for a long time during which no words were spoken between the three warriors. Aanya went through the pouches on her left leg and muttered quietly checking her supplies. Jason checked his first aid kid periodically, but mostly sat in silence and looked at his hands. Juniper continued searching for news of Zane on her cell but couldn't find anything. They had left Aquilo's palace around one o'clock and they arrived at the hospital at around two thirty.

They got out of the car and walked inside and were greeted by the receptionist, "Hello-" he cut off his sentence when he looked up and saw Juniper, "Ah apologies Your Highness, how can I help you?"

"We need to see the boy who was brought in today, long caramel hair and a scar tracing the left side of his face."

"Ah yes, he was brought in about three hours ago," said the receptionist, "He hasn't woken up. From what I've heard he's not hurt too badly but he won't be going anywhere for a while."

"That's fine I just need his room number if that's alright?" Juniper replied.

"Of course, Princess." the receptionist typed on his computer, "He's in room 205."

"Great, thank you," Juniper said, she faced Jason and Aanya, "Come on."

The group walked down the hall and went to the second floor. They found Carmine's room and walked in to see the couple whose roof he crashed through. James got to his feet and dropped to a kneel, while his wife stayed seated with a dumbfounded look on her face.

Juniper's gaze immediately shifted to an unconscious Carmine, "Jason, check him out." He nodded, and his eyes lit up as he looked over Carmine while Juniper went to talk to the couple, "Hello, Mr. and Mrs.Mousai, how are you I'm a fan of your work."

"Ah, well yes, thank you for your kind words, Your Highness," replied Ava.

"Mr. Mousai you don't have to..." Juniper said calmly.

He stood up and she saw his eyes, Juniper looked at Ava's and noticed that they were the same shades of green as in Carmine's heterochromia. She also noticed that James and Carmine had the same hair color. Juniper brushed it off as a coincidence and left it at that.

"So, if you don't mind, I wanted to ask about this boy. I happen to know him, and I was hoping you could tell me more about him crashing through your roof?"

Before they answered Jason spoke up, "Hey Junie, I looked him over and saw something this place might have missed."

"What did you find?" Juniper asked.

"I'm not sure but you should be able to heal it without any issue. It's not very big, or dangerous right now." Jason replied.

"Show me where."

Jason gently moved Juniper's hand over where the injury was, and she healed it. As soon as Juniper healed the injury Carmine shot up and started coughing violently. When he stopped coughing, he saw Juniper.

"Junie?" He said, his voice raspy.

"Yeah, it's me, Aanya and Jason are here too."

Carmine's expression was hard to read with his hair in his face, "Who's Jason?"

Jason sighed, "Hey, that's almost what Aanya said. I know I'm not important, but do you guys really need to rub it in like that?"

Carmine ignored him, "Aanya where are we?"

"Junie mentioned a kingdom called Terra," Aanya replied.

"Aanya do me a favor and catch Carmine up on the situation, Jason flag down a nurse or doctor to let them know Carmine's awake."

They both nodded, Jason, walked out of the room while Aanya started explaining the events of that day to Carmine while Juniper went to speak with Ava and James again.

"So, one thing I need to know is if Carmine had anything on him when he showed up."

James nodded, "He had a sword, we didn't know whether or not it was important, so we took it with us but left it in our car."

"Okay, can you tell me if anyone else was with him? I was already told this person didn't go with them, but I'm still concerned she might have." Juniper said as a doctor came in and started talking to Carmine.

"No, he was completely alone, in fact, the strangest part wasn't the fact a complete stranger fell through the ceiling while we were eating lunch in the other room it was the fact that he seemed strangely familiar." Ava said, with a twinge of embarrassment.

Juniper nodded and made a mental note about that when the doctor came over and started talking to them.

"So, we need to run a few more tests to make sure he's actually alright but we did find something strange in his system."

James tilted his head, "What did you find exactly?"

"We're not sure, but it's emitting a bit of radiation."

Juniper nodded and saw Carmine was facing away from her, so he held her hand open and summoned the tracker. In an instant, the tracker was in her hand, and he let out a very high-pitched yelp, and Jason started laughing.

"Dang, Carmine's got range!" Aanya said.

"You yelped at frequencies only dogs can hear," Juniper said.

"Shut up, you would have too if you felt what I just felt," Carmine snapped.

The group of warriors laughed. The doctors still needed to run their tests, so the group left to wait in the waiting room.

"So, when we leave, if you could return Carmine's sword that would be great," Juniper said.

"Yeah, I figured we would have to do that. It would be weird if we kept it," replied James, rubbing the back of his neck.

"I was also wondering if I could get a way to keep in touch, maybe figure out why he showed up around you?"

Ava and James froze when Juniper asked.

"Uhh sure, let's do that," Ava said after regaining her voice.

They exchanged phone numbers.

"If you ever need me or you have any questions let me know."

They nodded and all waited for Carmine to come back out. After about fifteen minutes Carmine came into the room and greeted the group again.

"So, we can leave now, right?" Carmine asked, "I'm kinda sick of this place."

"Carmine you've been here consciously for like twenty minutes," Aanya said, poking his cheek.

"I know I just don't really care, but where's my sword?" Carmine asked as he swatted Aanya's hand away.

"They've got your sword and you'll get it back."

Carmine shrugged and the group left the hospital. Ava got Carmine's sword from her car and returned it to Carmine. He thanked her, then turned and went to where Juniper, Aanya, and Jason were waiting for him.

"So where are we going now?" Carmine asked the group.

"We know where Circe is so we're going after her, then we're going to see about finding Zane."

Juniper said while showing the driver where they needed to go.

"Where are we going?" Carmine asked, "I'd like to see my girlfriend soon."

"We're going to the kingdom on the other side of the next kingdom over." Juniper said as they were getting into the car, "We're in Terra right now and we're going to Vulcan, so we have to go through Oxidane, but it might be faster to go through Providence City."

"So how long will it take us to get there?"

"If we go through Providence then maybe two hours but if we go through Oxidane, if traffic is good three hours maybe three and a half."

Carmine nodded and the car started moving down the street. The ride to Vulcan castle town was just as quiet; the driver took them through Providence instead of Oxidane so they could get to Circe in the shortest amount of time. Juniper wanted to start a conversation but didn't know what to say. The two-hour drive went by slowly, but they eventually made it to the first precinct in Vulcan castle town.

They walked into the building and started talking to the officer at the front desk, "Excuse me, officer?"

The officer who was taking a drink of water almost choked when she spoke, "Good afternoon

Your Highness. How can I help you?"

"We need to speak with a girl who was brought in about-" Juniper checked the time, "four hours ago, um blue eyes, brown and pinkish-purple hair, and freckles."

"Well, I can call the captain and ask but I'm not sure if she'll want anyone to see her."

"Well, if it's alright may we know why she was arrested?" Juniper asked.

"Umm, she crashed through a window and got to her feet unharmed by some miracle, then when a couple of our detectives tried talking to her, she ran and you know what happens if you run from the police, so when they tried to stop her, she kicked one of them in the knee,"

"So she did feel threatened," Juniper said to herself.

"Pardon?" said the officer.

"Ah nothing, please continue."

"After that, a small fight broke out, but the officers managed to put a pair of handcuffs on her and confiscate her weapons, so now she's either being processed or she's in the interrogation room."

"Okay, but can we speak with her?" Carmine said rather aggressively.

"Carmine please calm down," Aanya said, putting her hand on her friend's shoulder.

Carmine looked down and Juniper noticed Aanya wasn't wearing her leg holster and her jacket was zipped up, probably to hide her shoulder holster. Carmine didn't seem to have his sword on him, and Juniper wondered if he could turn things he was holding invisible.

"While he did say that aggressively, he is right, we do need to see her." Juniper said.

"I'll call our captain and she'll see what she can do, Your Highness," replied the officer.

"Thank you, sir."

She backed up and saw Carmine was tense and Aanya was trying to calm him down.

"So, he's calling his captain and she'll see about letting us talk to Circe."

"Alright, but what's with them calling you Your Highness?" Carmine asked.

"Yeah, I wanted to ask too but didn't know how to bring it up," Aanya continued.

Jason looked at her, "So you know I'm the queen from the Facility, but this isn't the Facility, but I'm still what you would call a high rank, I'm the princess of Flora the next kingdom over." Juniper said.

"So how did you become the princess?" asked Aanya.

"I'm a part of the Flora royal family, there isn't a ranking system if you're not born royal the only way to become one is to marry into the family."

Carmine nodded and the police captain walked over, "So you can speak with her but she can't leave unless we get her full name so we can finish processing her."

"She won't tell you her name, I can tell you that now." Juniper told the captain.

"Well, she told us her first name is Circe but she won't tell us her last name. She's claiming she doesn't remember it."

"Well, she actually doesn't, it's been maybe thirteen years since anyone has used it, the same goes for me and Aanya hasn't heard hers in eleven," said Carmine, trying to help.

"Why in the five kingdoms would someone forget their own last name?"

"I don't mean to sound disrespectful, but he did just explain why she might have forgotten," Juniper said.

The captain nodded and gestured for them to follow her. They followed her to the second floor where they saw Circe talking to a detective. When she saw Carmine her face lit up.

"Carmine! You're okay," Circe said happily.

She almost got up and the detective sitting next to her stopped her and held her in her chair, "Circe you're not going anywhere," she said.

The detective had light brown hair pulled

into a neat bun and rich brown eyes. Her badge was clipped to her belt, and she had a tattoo of a frequency wave on her wrist.

"Hello, Detective-?" Juniper started.

"Donna, Olivia Donna," said the Detective.

"Well Detective Donna, I'm deeply sorry for all the trouble my friend here has caused," Juniper said, gently.

"Oh, it's quite alright Princess, she didn't cause any major damage or injuries," Olivia replied looking over at Circe, who avoided eye contact.

Juniper was about to ask a few more questions when another detective walked over. She had the same tattoo Olivia had in the same spot, she also had black hair in a pixie cut with light blue eyes and her badge hung around her neck.

"Hey, Olivia I'm heading out to check the lead about the recent murder. We might have found some of the killer's DNA," said the new detective.

"Okay, Emma see you tonight, love you," replied Olivia.

Emma walked over to the elevator and stepped in to leave as Juniper turned back to Olivia.

"So, you have a wife?" Juniper asked.

"Yeah, I do," replied Olivia, she started rubbing the tattoo on her wrist.

"So, what's with that tattoo?" Juniper asked, trying to find another way to get Circe out of here without breaking the law.

"Well, my wife and I moved to Vulcan from Terra to adopt a baby girl whose parents died in a car crash and about five years after, she disappeared so in memory of her, we got the frequency of her laugh tattooed on our wrists."

"That's awful, how long has she been missing now?" Juniper asked, a twinge of sadness in her voice.

"It's been about thirteen years. I'd say if she's still alive she about eighteen now."

Juniper thought about it and noticed that if you look at that story from the child's perspective, if they didn't die then it matched what happened to the warriors from the Facility.

"Unfortunately, we weren't the only ones this happened to, and the others had the same calling card. I suppose we also didn't have it the worst out of everyone." Olivia said, shifting her attention to a file on her desk.

"Well, I'm sorry to hear that, but back to my friend, she has been attending a-" Juniper paused, she didn't want to explain the Facility and needed a new word, "A boarding school, and hasn't been using her last name so she forgot it."

"As much as I would love to help you Princess,

I do need her full name to write a report," Olivia said with a shrug.

"I wish I could give it to you," replied Juniper.

Juniper wondered if she should give the officer a fake name, but since that was illegal she decided against it.

"You said you didn't have it the worst among those whose children had vanished. Can you tell me more about them?" Juniper questioned.

"Due to all of them being cold cases and some being from other kingdoms I can't tell you much other than this, a small portion of us started a support group," Olivia said quietly, "We're meeting for a monthly lunch in the big park in Providence, it's tomorrow at one. It was the only day all of us were available. Come and you can ask them your questions there."

"Alright sure I'll see about being there but back to Circe, is there anything else we can do since we don't know her full name only her first?"

"I suppose because this was her first offense, she didn't cause any major league damage or injuries, she felt threatened and was only defending herself, and she has royalty vouching for her I can let this slide and she can be let go with a warning."

"Oh, thank you, you have no idea how great that is!" Juniper exclaimed.

Olivia turned and wrote something down on a piece of paper, "Here's my number if you have any questions about that support group and tomorrow's meetup." Olivia turned back to her computer, "As soon as I'm done with this report you can be on your way."

Juniper nodded and took the group downstairs to wait for Circe. They waited quietly for an hour when Olivia escorted Circe back to the first floor where they were waiting by the door. Aanya had been teasing Carmine about his scream from earlier, while Jason stood behind them trying to be invisible.

"Alright, you're good to go." Olivia said as Circe walked over to Carmine.

"Okay, but one more question, you said this had happened to multiple people, and I've noticed a correlation between this group and yours. Did any of the members say they met a guy named Zane, black hair, icy blue eyes, a claw mark scar over his left eye, and only communicates through sign language?" Juniper asked Olivia.

Olivia rubbed the back of her neck, "Actually, yes a friend of mine who lost her brother. Her name's Belle she said a guy matching that description showed up at her house around the same time Circe showed up here, but she didn't say anything about the sign language. She might not know," Olivia answered.

"Oh, that's great, would it be possible to visit her tonight, it's getting late, but I'd rather find Zane soon than leave him alone for an entire night," Juniper said, "Also did Circe have a bow and a quiver of arrows and would it be possible to get them back?"

"Yeah, I'll grab the bow and arrow, but you should know where Belle lives. She's the heir to Hydro-meds, the company of the Bardot family," Olivia said, adjusting the badge on her belt.

"The Bardot family!? That's the wealthiest family in the five kingdoms," Juniper said a little surprised, "They had a son?"

"Yeah, but he, like my daughter and a few other people's children vanished and was never found, but I could let her know you're coming by later," replied Olivia.

"That would be great thanks, but now we need the bow and arrow."

"Yeah, I'll go grab it."

Olivia walked off and Juniper turned around just in time to see Circe and Carmine kiss, "I was worried about you." Circe said gently, her hands still on his face.

"Yeah, I crashed through a roof and ended up in a hospital," he replied looking away.

"He woke up and during a conversation with

the doctor he yelped like a little kid," Aanya said with a smirk.

"Oh yeah it was hilarious," Jason followed.

"Why did you yelp?" Circe asked.

Juniper shrugged and Carmine glared at Aanya. Circe turned and started laughing at her boyfriend. While Circe's back was turned, Juniper used her power to remove the tracker in her brand. After a minute Juniper had the tracker in her hand and Circe was rubbing her shoulder blade. While Circe and Aanya teased Carmine, Olivia came back with Circe's bow and arrows and returned them to Juniper.

"Enjoy the rest of your evening Your Highness, and see you tomorrow."

Juniper passed the weapons to Circe, "Thank you for all your help, Detective Donna."

"It's not a problem. That is my job after all, anyway I'll be heading home now."

They said their goodbyes and walked out to their cars. It was about six o'clock and they now had a two-hour ride to the Bardot family house then another one through Providence back to Flora.

"Alright group, we've got a long night ahead of us, we're heading to Oxidane then back to my home. It's going to be about four to four and a half hours if all goes well."

Chapter 12

The two-hour ride to the Bardot family estate was just as quiet as the previous drives of that day. Circe sat with her bow in her lap and her quiver on the floor next to her feet. She and Carmine were sitting next to each other. Carmine had his sword back and he had it leaning on his leg and Juniper hadn't managed to ask if he had turned it invisible at the police precinct. Aanya sat looking out the window with a tired, longing look, while Jason stared at the floor around his feet, nervous to be so close to so many high rankers.

When they arrived at the estate the driver rang the buzzer and the gate opened. They drove up the driveway and were in front of the house. Circe shouldered her bow and arrows, Carmine's sword seemed to have vanished again, and Aanya zipped up her jacket hiding her gun leaving the other in the car.

"Carmine, are you turning your sword invisible?" Juniper asked while they walked to the door.

"Yeah, I can turn things invisible, but I have to be able to carry it." Carmine replied, "Here see." His sword shimmered and appeared in its sheath tied to his belt.

"Circe, would you be okay with Carmine holding on to your weapons, so we don't scare the people living here?"

"Yeah, I can do that." Circe said, taking off her bow and arrows.

She passed them to Carmine who slung them over his shoulder, as soon as he let go, they shimmered and disappeared. Juniper turned to the door, and it was opened by a butler. He had them follow him and he led them through hallways to an office space where the CEO of Hydro-meds Mark Bardot was waiting with his wife Eliza Bardot.

"Good evening Your Highness it's awfully late for a visit don't you think?" Mark started.

Juniper took a deep breath "Apologies, Mr. Bardot, however, we heard that one of our friends had arrived here earlier today and we were hoping you'd let him come with us."

"I don't mean to sound disrespectful, Princess however he did trespass on our property," Eliza said, a sly smile crept across her face, "Perhaps you'd like to discuss our letting this little mishap slide over dinner, you must be hungry from such a long drive here."

That sentence made Juniper nervous, the Bardot family was famously skilled at negotiating unfair terms to get more than they give. If the person they're negotiating with isn't careful they could lose way more money than necessary. The Bardot family had managed to successfully negotiate someone signing off their business to them, now they were negotiating with royalty. Juniper knew she had to be incredibly careful or else losing something she couldn't replace.

Juniper kept her nerves under control, "Dinner sounds wonderful thank you, however, we want to make sure the boy you have in custody is the one we're looking for."

"Very well he can join us for dinner as well," Mark said standing up.

Eliza told one of the staff to tell her daughter and the visitor to join them in the dining room. The group walked down the hall and arrived at the dining room where Juniper asked for a moment alone with her group.

"Take as much time as you need, just open this door when you're ready," Mark said, closing the door behind him.

"Alright, listen to me you four, this family is famous for negotiating unfair deals, and this time we're negotiating for Zane's freedom, they'll be asking a lot for that," Juniper stated sternly.

"So, let's take the first deal they give and never talk about it again," Aanya replied.

"Aanya this means we need to be so careful; we want Zane to come back with us, but we only want to give the bare minimum," Juniper said quietly, "We can't accept the first deal they give, they might expect us to do that, let me negotiate our terms."

The four warriors nodded, and Juniper turned to open the door. They walked in and saw Zane standing next to a girl around the age of twenty-four. Aanya almost ran straight to Zane, but Juniper discreetly held her back. Zane looked Juniper in the eyes then to Aanya and back to Juniper who shook her head.

"Well, she seemed excited to see our guest here." Mark remarked.

Aanya started signing while muttering what she was saying under her breath and Zane turned his attention to her hands, as soon as Aanya put her hands behind her back Zane signed back. The girl seemed intrigued by what was being signed like she could understand what was being said.

"Your Highness, this is our daughter Belle, she's the heir to our company. I'm sure you already know what we do," Mark said, gesturing to the girl who then curtsied.

"Yes of course Mr. Bardot, you produce and distribute medicine to the five kingdoms," Juniper said, in an attempt to flatter him, "It is the most famous company, with the largest net worth."

"Oh well thank you, but please save the flattery for another time, people have tried that as a negotiation tactic before," Mark said with a smirk.

Juniper realized just how tricky this was going to be. She knew if she made one slip up and said the wrong thing she would be on the wrong end of a bad deal. They all sat down at the table as the food was brought out. There was enough food for everyone, and Juniper wondered how they had the foresight to make this much when as far as Juniper was aware they had only been told she was coming, not an exact number.

"Well, I certainly hope this food is up to your standards, Your Highness." Eliza said, settling into her chair.

Juniper nodded, "I hope so as well, but please let discuss terms so Zane can return with us."

"Now now, princess, let's not rush things, it's only eight fifteen, we'll have plenty of time for these dealings after dinner," Mark spoke with an underlying tone of deceit.

Something that Juniper knew perfectly about

business was that lying was common among businessmen. They lied to get what they wanted. Good businessmen could lie, get what they asked for, and leave no trail with completely legal trades. Not many people could outwit an experienced CEO no matter their social status.

"Oh well, I promised my father to be home tonight, and it's a two-hour drive through Providence. I'd really rather get through this quickly to make sure my parents aren't too worried," Juniper mentioned, trying to have the negotiation happen on her terms.

As soon as she said that Mark lowered the glass he was about to take a drink from and set it down on the table, "Well, we wouldn't want His Majesty worried about his daughter now would we."

"Oh, not at all, so very well princess, we'll negotiate now." Eliza said, "My husband and I noticed something the moment you entered our home, if you want us to release this boy and drop all charges of trespassing, we only want one thing."

Juniper knew if they were only asking for a single item it had to be worth it, "What are you asking for?"

Mark smiled and leaned forward, "That pendant, we've never seen one like it. It must be one of a kind and fairly expensive."

The silver pendant hung heavily around her

neck; she knew she couldn't give it up. It was the last thing she had of Aiden. It kept them connected so she could be sure of seeing him again. But as soon as that thought came to her mind, she got mad at herself for thinking that. She was engaged and he had tried to kill her then abandoned her.

The group looked at her except for Zane who kept his eyes down, "I'm sure this is a fair trade, after all this boy you're after is worth much more than a pendant like that, you don't want him getting arrested and serving hard time for thievery and trespassing do you?" Eliza uttered, "Besides I have a pair of earrings that would go amazingly well with that silver chain."

Juniper stared right into Eliza's frozen blue eyes, "From what I remember you had a son but he disappeared maybe twelve years ago."

Eliza leaned back while Mark turned to Juniper, "How did you find out about that?" Mark asked, "And what are you saying?"

"What I'm saying is almost nobody knows, and you want to keep it that way." Juniper stated, "You know how it would look if everyone knew someone managed to break into your house and kidnap your son, how about instead of me turning over my pendant you let us take Zane with us and we keep this whole thing including the kidnapping of your son our little secret."

Eliza was speechless while Mark was scared, Juniper could tell, "You wouldn't dare."

"Try me."

The princess and the CEO were looking right into each other's eyes from either side of the table, Juniper showing no emotion while Mark was struggling to keep his hidden.

"So Mr. Bardot, do we have a deal?" Juniper said, holding her hand out.

Mark took a quivering breath and shook her hand, "I accept your terms."

He released her hand and Juniper stood up with a proud smile on her face, "Thank you for your hospitality but we best be on our way, Aanya please tell Zane to follow us."

Aanya nodded with a huge smile on her face. She quickly signed to Zane to follow. As soon as he read her signs he smiled too, stood up and walked with the group out the door and to the car. Before he got in Juniper removed his tracker. He did nothing more than wince then they all climbed into the car and set off for Juniper's palace.

One two-hour drive later the group arrived back at Juniper's home. Juniper led them through the hallways into the throne room where her parents were waiting.

"That took a lot longer than expected." Marcus said, as they walked in.

"I'm sorry dad there were a lot of things that needed to be sorted out, but I did find the rest of the group and they're all okay," Juniper replied, gesturing to the group behind her.

Circe had her bow and arrow back on her shoulder, while Carmine's sword was strapped to his back rather than tied to his belt, and Aanya had both her holsters on. Jason and Zane didn't carry weapons, but they all looked tired. It had been a long day and Juniper was sure they just wanted to sleep.

"So, what are their powers, we've already seen those two but what about the rest of you?" Alice asked, glancing at all of them.

"A quick rundown, Carmine can turn himself and anything he can carry invisible, Circe can shapeshift into a phoenix, and Zane has cryokinesis," Juniper said, pointing to who she was talking about.

Circe stepped forward, "Would you like us to demonstrate?"

Marcus and Alice looked at each other, "If you don't cause any damage then sure," Marcus said for the two of them.

Aanya, Jason, and Juniper backed out of the way while Carmine and Circe moved forward. Aanya signed to Zane what was going on and he stepped forward lining himself up with the others. Zane picked up his foot and slammed it against the floor which caused a layer of ice to spread quickly over it. As he exhaled you could see his breath; he then knelt down and pressed his hand flat against the ice which splintered and disappeared as fast as it had come.

Circe stepped in front of the two boys while holding her arms out, around the base of her neck they saw feathers grow and ruffle. After a few seconds where Circe had been standing was a three-foot-tall bright red bird with hints of pink in the under feathers, she spread her wings showing a wingspan of around seven feet and she took off flying gracefully around the room. They watched as her feathers shimmered in the light she landed in front of Juniper's parents, keeping her wings spread out and bowed before shifting back to human form and backing up to the group.

Carmine then took the stage; he unstrapped his sword from his back and drew it from its sheath. They watched as the sword he was holding shimmered and vanished then Carmine did the same. They heard the sound of him sheathing his sword but couldn't hear his footsteps. They waited for a few seconds before he reappeared behind the king and queen kneeling on the ground. He stood up and walked back over to the group and turned his attention back to Juniper's parents.

"Well, I'd be a fool to deny that was impressive, but how did you get these powers?" Marcus asked.

"We don't know we've just always had them," Carmine replied, "We have spent a good portion of our lives working with them and other methods of fighting to become stronger."

Alice noticed that Aanya was acting as an interpreter for Zane, because he couldn't read lips and didn't know what the others were saying, "I'm sorry what is she doing?"

"Zane is deaf, and as his girlfriend I've taken it upon myself to be fluent in sign language so he can know what's going on."

"Alright then, well we've got plenty of room here for you all so, Juniper can you take them to the guest rooms for the night I'm sure you all would love to get some sleep." Marcus said, pointing to the side door.

"I'll do that, dad." Juniper turned around, "Okay just follow me and I'll get you situated."

Juniper led them through the palace and gave them individual rooms and took Jason back to the one he had been using. After they were all in their rooms Juniper went to hers to change. As Juniper pulled her hair into a messy bun her focus shifted to something she saw in her mirror, on her nightstand was a small envelope.

Juniper picked it up and opened it, "It's the DNA test results," she whispered to herself.

Juniper looked at the results to see the names of his parents. His mother was Kristen Blakely, which wasn't a surprise to Juniper; but the name of his father confused Juniper, the name under biological father was Sephtis Kai. The name made Juniper uneasy. It was familiar but she couldn't figure out why. Juniper knew she should go to sleep but had to know why she recognized the name. She searched it up on her computer and discovered he was the last person Kristen was commissioned to kill before she was caught. That struck Juniper as odd due the fact he was killed a year before Aiden was born so how could he have been his father?

"This makes no sense," Juniper murmured to herself, "There's no way this man is dead he has to still be alive somewhere."

Juniper dug a little deeper to find a picture of him, when she found one, she almost screamed. Juniper turned off her computer, went to her bed and fell onto it.

"Five kingdoms, this is bad." Juniper murmured, "I need to rescue Aiden soon."

Chapter 13

Juniper woke up the next morning and went back to her computer to make sure what she had seen the night before was real. She was disappointed to see it was, Juniper knew she'd have to tell Aiden. Juniper wasn't sure he'd believe her, so she printed the screen. She folded the paper over the DNA test paper and put it back in the envelope when there was a knock at her door.

"Just a minute." Juniper said. She hid the envelope under her computer and ran to open the door, when she met her mother's eyes, "Hey mom, good morning."

Alice looked at her daughter, "Are you okay? You seem tense."

Juniper glanced around and saw her computer in her peripheral vision still on the screen with Sephtis Kai, she turned around, closed the tab and turned off her computer, "I'm fine."

"That doesn't look very fine to me," her mother replied, crossing her arms and leaning on the door frame.

"It's nothing important, it's just something I needed research on for the group."

That wasn't completely untrue, it had to do with Aiden who Juniper considered part of the group. She still needed a way to get back to the Facility otherwise this information was useless to her. Juniper also remembered they were going to Providence Garden to meet that support group today.

"Hey mom, while we were getting all the people yesterday, we were told about this support group that might be able to help us. They're holding a meet up in Providence Garden. Would it be possible for us to go?" Juniper asked.

"Are you sure? I mean you were gone all of yesterday just trying to find these people and now you want to go out and meet a group of people you don't even know?"

Juniper knew how her request might have sounded, "I know it's a crazy request, but I feel like this group might have a connection to the group I went after yesterday's parents."

"You also still have those other people after you, wouldn't they want to hurt you?" Alice asked a twinge of worry in her voice.

Juniper felt bad, this was hard for her, she couldn't imagine what this was like for her family and friends that didn't know the full story. Juniper had kept so much from them, they didn't know how to feel, she understood they were scared but Juniper couldn't just keep away from the issue at hand she had to help.

"Mom, I know you're scared but I have to deal with these problems. I need to help them."

"Okay, but please don't be out too late. Try to be back before dinner."

"I will mom."

Alice turned and walked out of the room closing the door behind her and Juniper felt the bandages around her torso, "I should probably change these, only problem is that I don't know how."

But Juniper knew who did. She left her room and walked down the hallway to Jason's room and knocked on the door.

Jason opened his door, "Yes, Junie."

Juniper tried for a smile and made a vague gesture to her back, Jason thankfully understood what she meant and invited her into the room. He went into his bathroom to wash his hands and pull on some gloves. He walked behind her, and his eyes started glowing. He felt her back for a minute before pulling away.

"If you used your healing on it just a bit more then you should be fine."

"Thanks Jason, I'll handle that then.

Remember we are heading to Providence, we're leaving around eleven to get there on time, tell the others."

Jason nodded and Juniper went back to her room. As soon as Juniper closed the door behind her she did her best to reach her back and heal the wound. When she felt she couldn't heal it further she stopped and removed the bandages. She adjusted her stance so she could see the scar in the mirror. There was now a huge diagonal scar running from her right shoulder to her left hip. Juniper changed and went to the dining hall for breakfast.

As Juniper walked past all the rooms, she knocked on the doors to let them know where to go, being careful to let Aanya know she needed to help Zane out. When Juniper made it to the dining hall she waited outside, after a few minutes the whole group walked up to her.

"I'm impressed you could find it on your own."

Circe shrugged, "We didn't. Jason tracked you down using his power."

Jason nodded, and the group walked through the doors. Juniper's parents were having a conversation when her father shook his head, and her mother patted his arm.

"Hey dad, is there a problem?" Juniper asked.

"Yeah, there's good news and bad news. The good news you get to see your grandparents tomorrow, the bad news they're my parents not your mother's."

Juniper started to smile pitifully, she and her mother knew how he felt about his parents. They had never liked Alice and tended to ridicule Marcus for choosing to be with her. They were also traditionalists and really strict, if something was just off of perfect, they wouldn't let anyone hear the end of it.

"Oh dad, it's okay you'll be fine."

Carmine tapped Juniper on the shoulder, "Does he have a problem with his parents?"

"No, it's more they have a problem with his wife, they're strict and always though my mom wasn't good enough for him."

Juniper's father rubbed his temples, "They will never say anything to her face only passive aggressive comments and pulling me aside to tell me it's not too late to remarry."

They all sat down for breakfast. The Facility members didn't know how to make the meal not awkward. They kept their eyes on their plates, occasionally one would glance up but if someone looked at them, they would look down immediately. After a silent breakfast Juniper's parents had work to do so they left.

"Alright we are leaving for the meeting in Providence at eleven, the meet up is at one, but we do have a long drive to get there."

"So why exactly are we meeting with this group?" asked Zane with Aanya as a translator.

"They might have information on your parents, I'm sure you'd like to see them again."

They all seemed surprised about that. Juniper thought there was something strange about the people she met yesterday, she thought it might be because of how they talked about who showed up and where they were. The Mousais said that Carmine was strangely familiar, Detective Donna addressed the kidnapping of her daughter and it seemed alike to all the kidnapped children of the Facility, and Belle seemed to understand sign language based on her reaction to Zane and Aanya using it despite being able to hear and speak fully. All these interactions seemed just slightly off, and Juniper thought she might have figured out why.

"You do want to meet your families, don't you?" Juniper asked.

"Why would they want to meet us?" Carmine replied.

Circe nodded glumly, "We're not normal, we're outcasts anywhere but the Facility."

"That's at least what the Commander would

tell anyone who asked about the outside world," Aanya continued.

"We should still meet them; you never know what could happen," Juniper said.

They looked away from her, "Just because I remember my father that doesn't mean he'll want to meet me," Jason said, "I already made this point."

Juniper didn't know how to change their minds, but a servant came in holding a small box. She walked over to Juniper and handed her the box.

"Here are the hearing aids you ordered princess."

That caught everyone's attention, "Thank you," Juniper replied.

The servant bowed and left, everyone at the table looked at her. Their minds seemed to be racing but none of them could figure out what to say except for Zane who seemed more confused than anything.

Juniper looked at the box then passed it to Aanya, "Give this to Zane for me?"

Aanya looked at the box, "Uhh, sure."

Aanya handed the box to Zane and signed something after he took it. After Aanya stopped signing his eyes widened and looked at Juniper. Juniper smiled at him, he smiled back and opened the box. He picked up the hearing aids and put them on.

He sat for a minute before Aanya took a breath, "Zane can you hear me?"

Zane looked toward Aanya with tears in his eyes and nodded.

Everyone cracked a smile, "You can hear us, Zane?" Juniper asked.

Zane was starting to cry, he took a shaky breath and wiped the tears off his face, and nodded again.

They all smiled and started crying too. Zane was laughing and had a huge smile on his face. Aanya threw her arms around him, Carmine started clapping and Circe joined him, Jason was trying and failing to hide his smile, and Juniper just sat watching all of them also smiling.

"Alright, now we are going to that meet up, please stop trying to change my mind." Juniper said.

They all gave in to what Juniper said and left it at that.

"So, what do we do until then?" asked Jason.

"Explore, don't break anything or touch anything on the walls but we're leaving at eleven, so explore the palace until then. We've got two hours."

They all just kinda shrugged and nodded,

Juniper got up and left for her room. She decided to work on an outfit she could easily fight in if necessary. She looked through her closet and found a light breathable shirt that paired nicely with a skirt that wouldn't take long to adjust to a tear away skirt in case of a fight. She also found a decent sturdy pair of shorts. She changed into the shirt and shorts and attached her knife holster to the back. She then picked up the skirt and remade it to be easily taken off then put back on. She tested it and decided it worked. She left it on. Juniper went and redid her hair into a ponytail to keep it out of her face. Then she grabbed a different pair of shoes. As long as she didn't do anything reckless wearing the skirt nobody would be able to tell she was wearing combat boots. By the time she was done it was almost eleven, so she walked to the great hall holding her sword. She waited for a few minutes when the others arrived in the hall.

"Alright, are you guys ready to go?" Juniper asked.

"Yeah, let's go to this meet up," Circe replied.

They walked out to the car, while walking down the driveway Juniper handed Carmine her sword, who took it strapped to his back and turned it invisible. They all got into the car and the car started moving toward Providence. During the ride the one who was the most intrigued by everything was Zane, being able to hear for the first time in seventeen years was a new experience for him.

After a two-hour ride, they arrived at Providence gardens, they walked to the picnic area where Detective Donna said they'd be. As they walked over Juniper recognized all but four of them, the ones she recognized were the people who Carmine, Zane, and Circe had been dealing with the day before: Detectives Olivia and Emma Donna, Belle Bardot, and James and Ava Mousai. Of the people she didn't recognize one was a pretty woman with tawny skin, dark hair, and eyes that were a brownish purple, there was a couple with a daughter, the husband had dark purple eyes, brown hair, and chocolate skin, the wife had slightly lighter skin, with eyes that were dark brown and black hair, the daughter seemed to be perfect mix of the two with her mother's eyes and her father's hair. The final member of the group was a man who had light brown hair and eyes, with chocolate brown skin.

As they got closer Jason froze in his tracks, Juniper stopped and turned to him, "Hey, Jason are you okay?"

He looked like he'd seen a ghost, "It's my father."

"What?"

"That man, right there." Jason said, pointing to one of the group members, "He's my father."

Juniper looked at the support group, the man Jason had said was his father looked at Jason. The look in his eyes went from suspicion to surprise to disbelief. The man stood up and walked carefully toward Jason. The group looked at him strangely as he walked over. He stood in front of Jason and looked him in the eyes.

"Jason?" Said the man.

Jason took a step back and took a breath, "Yeah."

"Jason, is it really you?"

Jason nodded, "It's really me."

The man smiled, he stepped forward, reached out and touched Jason's shoulder, "You look just like your mother."

The man pulled Jason into a hug. Jason stood surprised before starting to cry and falling into his father's arms. Jason reciprocated the hug and they both stood there so happy to be reunited.

"Oh Jason, I missed you."

"I missed you too dad," Jason replied.

The tawny skinned woman stepped forward, "Nate who's this."

"Lucy, this is my son."

"Woah are you serious, this is your son? He's

really back?" Lucy asked.

Juniper smiled, "Apparently."

Lucy walked back to the table the group was at, they all watched the interaction between Nate and Jason smiling. Nate finally let go of Jason then faced Juniper.

"Your highness, I'm sorry if I offended you by that-" He started.

Juniper cut him off, "It's fine, he's your son it only makes sense you would go to him first." Juniper nodded toward the group, "Actually Detective Donna, Olivia Donna, told us this group might have connections about all of their parents. We were hoping you'd help."

"Oh of course Princess."

"But before we do that, Mr. and Mrs.Mousai, and Belle, could you come here? I want to speak with you." Juniper said as she made a gesture for her group to join the support group.

As the people she asked for walked over she grabbed Carmine and Zane's wrists to keep them by her, Carmine looked at her, "What are you doing?"

"You two need to be a part of this conversation as well."

Carmine and Zane stood on either side of Juniper, Belle was the first to ask why Juniper wanted to talk, "Not to sound impolite but why did you want to speak with us separately?"

"Just a minute Belle I'll get to you, but Mr. Mrs.Mousai please look at Carmine's eyes and tell me what you notice." Juniper said, pushing Carmine forward a little bit.

They seemed confused by the request, but did as Juniper asked and looked at his eyes. Carmine took a small step back. After a few minutes they looked back at Juniper and shrugged.

"Mr. Mousai, did you not notice that Carmine's left eye is the same shade of yellowish green as your wife's?" Juniper faced Ava, "And did you not notice that Carmine's right eye is the same shade of seafoam green, and his hair is the same caramel brown as your husband's?"

The couple looked at each other then back to Carmine, they seemed surprised.

"She's right." Ava said.

Juniper let them simmer in her revelation the turned to Belle, "I need you to envision your parents then compare what they look like to Zane, also yesterday he could only communicate via sign language but he got hearing aids this morning so he can hear you, but probably not speak fluently yet."

Belle looked at Juniper, "Why do you want me to do this?"

"You'll figure it out, but if I told you outright

what I'm thinking it would take away from my theory, you all should join us when you figure out what I'm getting at with my requests."

Juniper walked past them and joined the rest of the group at the picnic table. She glanced back at the five she left back there as they talked in confusion. The support group looked over at them as well.

"Your highness, what are you doing to them?" asked Nate.

"If they're smart, they'll figure it out," Juniper replied.

Aanya giggled, "Okay but that seems kind of mean."

Juniper shook her head at Aanya, "Anyway, can I meet all the members of this group?"

Lucy nodded, "Of course your highness, I'm Lucy Blaine, you've already met Oliva and Emma Donna, and Nate Campbell, but this is Celeste and John Quinn with their daughter Sofia."

"Well, it's a pleasure to meet you all, could we learn more about your group?"

"Of course, Princess," said Celeste, "My husband and I started this group shortly after our two oldest children were kidnapped, we had learned this had happened several times before to other people with the same calling card."

"We call our group the Checkered Rose

Support group, as the calling card was a black and white rose," John chimed in.

That last bit caught Juniper's attention, "You said a black and white rose, did the petals start white then fade to black?"

Lucy looked at Juniper strangely, "Yeah, how did you know?"

"It's not important. How did all of you find this group?" Juniper asked quickly, pushing her thoughts about the Facility away.

"Well, I found them because they were meeting at the library I work in," Lucy said.

"A few of my colleagues at the school I work at saw how bad I had been doing since losing Jason and they told me about it," Nate explained.

"Olivia and I were trying to solve the missing persons case for our daughter and learned about it," said Emma.

Juniper glanced behind herself to Zane and Carmine. From what she could see Belle had figured out what Juniper was getting at. Juniper saw her explain something to Zane before he wrapped his arms around her, after a few seconds they walked back to the group.

"Princess, how did you figure this out?" Belle asked.

"That Zane is your brother? You both have your mother's eyes," Juniper said.

The group seemed impressed by what Juniper had said. Lucy looked around the park area, she saw someone and instantly turned away.

"Don't look now, it's my ex," Lucy said.

Belle looked over her shoulder despite Lucy telling her not to, "Why is Elijah here, and he's with his wife and child."

Juniper looked back over to Carmine and the Mousai couple, they still hadn't put two and two together so Juniper gave them another hint.

"Hey!" Juniper shouted at them, "Don't you think there's a reason he looks so similar to you two."

They looked at Juniper, then back to Carmine when it finally clicked in their minds. The three started having a conversation where Carmine seemed to become uncomfortable answering their questions.

"How did you know about those relationships?" asked Nate, "You said it was the eyes for Zane and Belle but what about Ava and James with Carmine."

"The same reason: their eyes, it's something about family you can always tell just by the look in their eyes. Carmine has a strange far-off look of writer like his mother but also seemed to look at everything like it was music like his father."

"Well, if it isn't Lucy." said a voice behind

Juniper, "How did we end up in the same place?"

Lucy looked up at him, "What do you want Elijah? You'd never come over here unless you needed something."

"Oh no, I know two members of this group we trying to find our daughter I just wanted to ask if they finally found her after eleven years, you know since you let her go missing."

Juniper turned her head, "I'm sorry for interjecting, but it sounds like you're blaming your ex-wife for the kidnapping of your daughter, as if she let the kidnapper take her."

"Well, if she had stayed with her then nobody could have gotten our daughter alone, but alas she left her alone in the room."

Before Juniper could respond Aanya got defensive of Lucy, "Hey, stop it. Nobody chooses to be kidnapped and no parent certainly allows their child to be kidnapped."

"Who are you, trying to tell me off?" Elijah asked.

"Someone who you don't want angry," replied Aanya, standing up and facing him.

Aanya stood looking up at the man, he was two feet taller than her. Aanya was only four foot ten, so this man wasn't intimidated by her petite size. He looked down at her for a minute before backing up with a strange expression.

"What, did I intimidate you?" asked Aanya.

"No, that is impossible for you. But Lucy why didn't you tell me that our daughter was found."

Everyone at the table froze, Lucy looked at Elijah, "I didn't know she was, what are you talking about?"

"Her!" Elijah cried pointing at Aanya, "You can't tell me you don't see it; she looks just like our daughter did eleven years ago just a little taller."

"Well, isn't this just the sweetest. So many reunited families, next you'll say that Circe is the daughter of those detectives," said a girl from a nearby tree.

Chapter 14

Everyone stopped and looked toward the voice and Juniper froze, her hand went to her skirt. Juniper glanced over at Jason, he looked scared, but Juniper made eye contact with him and quickly looked to the side then back to him. He tensed up. Juniper mouthed the word 'run' at him. Jason nodded; he grabbed his father's wrist then moved. The speaker jumped toward Juniper, but the princess immediately tore off her skirt and wrapped it around the wrists of her attacker. Juniper managed to disarm her opponent and push her to the side.

"Well, that's a new move," said the attacker.

Juniper looked them right in the eye, "It's nice to see you too Erica, I'm surprised that you'd even come back. It's only been a day since you saw me last."

"Oh, what can I say, I'd like to get revenge for my brother's death, an eye for an eye and all that." Erica said, drawing a blade from a sheath on her thigh.

Juniper looked at her group, "Carmine, give me my sword, then take Circe and protect the support group, Aanya, Zane, I doubt the Commander would send Erica to fight alone, assume she has backup. Stay here and fight whoever else shows up."

All four of them nodded. Carmine took Juniper's sword off his back and tossed it to her after he grabbed his parents' wrists and pulled them toward where Jason ran. Circe ordered the rest of the group to come with her. Zane and Aanya ran to either side of the fight to wait for any backup that Erica might have.

"You don't think you could take multiple of us on at once?" Erica jeered.

Juniper drew her sword and shifted her footing for a fight. Erica smirked and twirled the knife in her hand. Erica shifted on her feet, she rushed forward and faced a front attack then moved to the side, Juniper managed to barely block the attack. Keeping most of her focus on Erica, Juniper saw someone in the bushes but didn't get a good look. Erica jumped toward Juniper, but Juniper locked the blade of Erica's knife on her sword. Juniper tried to hold her sword in place, but Erica was strong, she forced Juniper to lose her grip and managed to cut Juniper's shoulder. Erica drew her blade back and jabbed it forward to stab Juniper, Juniper dropped toward the ground and swept Erica's feet out from under her. The knife flew from Erica's grasp and Juniper caught it.

"Smooth moves." Erica said, getting to her feet.

Juniper backed up tossing the knife aside, "I learned from the best, didn't I?"

Juniper glanced to the side and saw Aanya fighting a guy wearing a strange mask while Zane fought a guy who seemed to be dodging his ice flawlessly. While Juniper was distracted Erica kicked Juniper, knocking her to the ground. Juniper tried to get to her feet, but Erica lifted up her foot and brought it down off Juniper's back right between her shoulder blades.

Juniper looked up and saw news crews coming to film the fight, with police sirens blaring over a nearby hill. Erica was about to kick Juniper again, but she rolled out of the way, got to her feet, and ran down the path. As she ran, she heard Erica shouting behind her. Juniper ran as fast as she could through some trees. She moved around them, but something grabbed her and yanked her to the side. Erica ran right past where Juniper was now hiding her back pressed against a stranger who had one arm holding her in place with the other hand covering her mouth.

Juniper pulled against her captor's grip, drew her knife, and held it against his throat, "If you think just because I'm... Aiden?"

Aiden stood with his back pressed against the tree and his hands up while Juniper's knife pressed against his throat, smirking, "How about a thank you for stopping Erica from stabbing you."

Juniper glared at him and lowered her blade, "I'm going to end you for that stunt you pulled back at the palace."

Aiden started laughing, "Hey relax I'm okay, I was sent here to avoid you and find the other royals."

"They've been gone a day; how does the Commander already know they're missing?"

"I don't know he just does. He's gotten worse since we left, it's only been three days I know but, something changed."

"What do you mean?"

Aiden looked over his shoulder, "He's been more irritable. Maybe it's the paranoia of me trying to escape again but, he's been keeping me back where I grew up, not letting me go back to the main area. He's also looking for someone and planning to take 'her' back but won't say who she is." Aiden said.

"Are you worried about him or you?"

"I'm not sure, I'm scared he might kill me, but he also raised me. I don't know if I'd consider him family but he's the closed thing I've got."

Juniper looked up at him, she never noticed how good-looking he was when he was nervous, "Stop thinking like that you've got a fiancé," she muttered to herself.

"What was that?"

"N-nothing, but Aiden I've got something to tell you-" Juniper started.

"Oh, A, you're not disobeying the Commander's orders, are you?" Erica said from the trees.

She swung down with a knife in her hands, Aiden immediately yanked Juniper behind him and grabbed Erica's arm pushing her to the ground. Before she could get up, he pinned her down and placed both hands on her shin and twisted it with a sickening crack breaking her leg.

Erica cried out in pain as Aiden got up, He looked down at her, "You know I didn't want to do that right?"

"Oh please." Erica spat, "You killed my brother so now you're going to kill me too."

Juniper knelt beside Erica, "We're not going to kill you, and we didn't kill Eylam. You saw me trying to heal him, The Commander stabbed him and left before anyone else saw him."

The three of them heard footsteps behind the trees. Juniper tried to get to her feet but the blood loss from the cut on her shoulder and the kick to her back caused her to stumble. Aiden caught her and helped her lean on a tree for support then pulled a pistol from a holster on his hip. He stepped closer to where the footsteps were coming from, someone stepped out into the clearing and Aiden held the gun out keeping them where they were standing.

The girl who stepped out was John and Celeste Quinn's thirteen-year-old daughter. She stumbled back when she saw the pistol pointed at her, "Woah I'm here looking for the princess. The police wanted to see her and ask about the group she was with."

Juniper looked at her, "You're not hurt are you, you didn't get caught in the fights going on over there?"

"No, the police are currently trying to break them up and news people are trying to get coverage, but we need you back."

"Alright..." Juniper paused, "I'm sorry I forgot your name."

"Sofia."

"Alright Sofia, I need you to tell Jason where we are."

"Um but the police are having trouble with

the fights, I was lucky to get safely past them." Sofia muttered.

"Sofia, try to get back to your parents and we'll be right behind you but if we don't get there after five minutes send Jason back in our direction."

Sofia nodded and ran back to her parents. Juniper grabbed the cut on her arm and healed it, she then did the same to her back. After moving her hand away, she immediately felt light-headed; Juniper stumbled to the side and caught herself on the tree.

"Hey, are you okay?" Aiden asked as he put his pistol away.

"Yeah, healing just really takes it out of me." Juniper pushed herself upright and looked at Erica, "Pick her up we need to break up those fights."

Aiden nodded, he knelt and picked up Erica. Juniper and Aiden went in the direction Sofia had come from and walked onto a grassy plane covered in streaks of ice and blood splatter. Juniper looked for Aanya and Zane, she walked over the green and saw Zane supporting Aanya with blood dripping down the side of his face. Aanya was coughing and looked really sick. Aiden pointed over where Zane was directing his power and Juniper saw the boy Aanya was fighting earlier had ditched his mask and was unconscious on the ground while the other one was glaring at Zane. The police had managed to stop them from doing anything else.

"Zane, is Aanya okay?"

Zane was gasping for air and Juniper noticed frost creeping up his fingertips and the side of his face. Zane shook his head and pointed at the unconscious boy.

"What did he do?"

Zane tapped his lips with one finger and pointed at the unconscious boy again, "Poison."

Aiden stepped forward, "Ben, stand down and put Don's mask back on him so he doesn't poison anyone else, then return home with him."

The one still on his feet reluctantly nodded and did as he was told. Juniper walked over to Aanya and pressed her hands to Aanya's forehead, Juniper healed Aanya and almost collapsed in exhaustion. Juniper was already weary after her fight with Erica and healing herself, she was starting to expend more energy than she had. Aanya's breathing steadied and her eyes fluttered open.

Aanya fixed her gaze on Juniper, "Hey, are you okay? Where's Erica?"

"Woah Aanya slow down there, you were poisoned I just healed you, and I'm alright just tired."

Zane looked down at her, and motioned the shoulder she was leaning on for her to move if she could, Aanya stood up and took her arm off Zane.

"Zane, is your head alright? That looks like an awful lot of blood," Juniper asked.

Zane nodded, "A?"

"Son of a-" Aiden swore, "Use my name!"

"Okay, have you been waiting to say that?" Carmine asked, and Aiden shot him a look, "Dang, alright Aiden it is then."

"Aiden, why are you carrying Erica?" Aanya asked.

"Erica was trying to kill us, so I broke her leg."

One of the police officers made his way to the group, "Excuse me, Your Highness, but do you know these people?"

"Yes sir, I do know this group of people." Juniper said struggling to her feet, "They're my friends please forgive their behavior they were only defending themselves and the support group over there."

"Well alright then. Does he need an ambulance? He's still bleeding," the officer said, looking at the side of Zane's face.

Zane looked at the officer, "I'm fine."

"Jason come here." called Juniper.

Jason walked down the hill, "What do you need?"

"Check the wound on Zane's head then help us with Erica."

Jason turned and looked at Zane. As Jason's eyes started glowing, he reached into his pocket and pulled out his first aid kit. Jason gingerly touched the side of Zane's face and moved his hair to reveal a gross wound. As Jason looked over the wound Zane winced. Jason bandaged the wound then turned to Erica, his eyes still glowing.

As Jason splinted Erica's leg, he said, "Both will be alright, the break in Erica's leg was a clean one and the wound on Zane's head looked worse than it actually was."

The support group walked down the hill and met the warriors at the bottom, "Okay what is going on?" Nate asked.

"It's a long story." Jason said quietly.

While Jason did his best to explain what was going on a knife fell from its sheath on the back of Erica's belt. Juniper knelt and picked it up, the blade was silver and stained with blood.

"Erica, what is this?" Juniper asked, showing her the knife.

"Eylam's murder weapon." Erica mumbled.

Celeste walked forward, "I'm sorry you said her name is Erica?"

Juniper looked at Celeste, then to her husband, "One of your missing children's names is Erica, isn't it?"

John walked forward as well, "Yeah how did you know."

Juniper looked at John's purple eyes, "Just like theirs." Juniper muttered, "And your missing daughter had a twin brother, right?"

"You're starting to sound creepy because you're right again," Celeste replied.

"In the five years before they went missing, they had their father's eyes and I've only met two people with that shade of purple," Juniper said.

The couple looked at each other, "What do you mean?" Celeste asked.

"I'm sorry." Juniper whispered, "I'm truly sorry you couldn't meet your son again, but you can see your daughter." Juniper continued nodding toward Erica.

The couple understood what Juniper meant. They took a step back and looked at Erica, Erica looked over at them and glared.

Aiden looked uncomfortable, "I feel like I'm in the way."

John reached out and grabbed Erica's arms. Aiden let her down from his arms, Erica lost her balance but with John holding her steady she stood up on one foot. Celeste touched Erica's cheek, as Celeste's fingertips grazed Erica's face she flinched away. Sofia stood awkwardly behind her parents looking at the strange eighteen-year-old girl.

Celeste cupped Erica's face in her hand and Erica didn't flinch away this time, "Oh, Erica look how you've grown up."

John looked at Erica, "What happened to your brother, why did Princess Juniper say we couldn't meet him?"

As soon as the question left John's mouth tears welled up in Erica's eyes, she fell into her father's arms sobbing. As Erica cried, Celeste put an arm over her back. Juniper looked at the group watching this all unfold, Nate put an arm around Jason, Belle glanced over at Zane who was holding onto Aanya tightly while Lucy stood next to them. Carmine stood by his parents and Circe held onto his hand, Olivia and Emma put a hand on Circe's shoulders. Juniper turned back to Erica, who had never looked so at peace.

Juniper was about to try to speak with Aiden when her phone started ringing, she reached into her back pocket and answered, "Hello?"

"Junie, what's this on the news about you getting into a fight?" asked a voice on the other line.

Juniper knew whose voice this was, "Elaine, sorry what?"

"On the news, it says in Providence Gardens,

Element Hill, Flora's Princess Juniper Ayer is fighting a girl while a few other people are fighting nearby."

"Right, the news people showed up, how did I forget them?" Juniper said looking over her shoulder at them, "Listen, Elaine, I'm fine. Before you ask any questions, I can't answer, I'll talk to you later."

She heard Elaine protesting something about Aeolus being worried about her, and Juniper hung up. Aiden gestured for her to speak with him away from the group.

"Aiden, I need to tell you something."

"Sorry Juniper it'll have to wait, I need to go back."

"No Aiden, listen this is important," Juniper protested.

Aiden looked away, "I don't have time, I really need to get back before the Commander makes me."

Juniper sighed, "Be safe, don't die before I come back for you."

Aiden smiled, "I'll try, see you soon."

Aiden turned and ran back to the trees, Juniper walked glumly back to the group. She saw Elijah arguing with Lucy, Aanya seemed to be getting upset with the argument, so Juniper went to see what all the fuss was about. As she walked past Erica, she removed her tracker.

Juniper broke the tracker in her hand then got the attention of everyone in the group with a loud sharp whistle, "What are you two arguing about?"

"I was just trying to tell her that Aanya should live with me, I've got a steady job and a family," Elijah said.

"And I told him no," Lucy replied.

Aanya looked at them, "Do I get a say in all this?"

Juniper rolled her eyes, "I'm sorry but with everything going on none of them are going back to their families quite yet, they need to stay together," Juniper looked at the rest of the group, "All of them are staying with me."

"But they're our children," commented Ava.

"They were also raised together and need to stay that way, for now, they're all in danger and it's not a good idea to separate them."

The support group seemed disappointed and Juniper didn't find that strange. She was also disappointed that she couldn't let her friends go with their families but with the Commander still after them, she knew letting them leave would put their lives in danger.

"I'm truly sorry that I can't let them go with you, but we need to get back so Zane, if you could help Erica."

Zane nodded and picked up the girl. The warriors followed Juniper back to her car. The group got in and left for the Flora palace.

As they rode along Juniper noticed Erica give her a death glare from time to time but would never say anything. Jason sat next to her keeping a hand on her shoulder which seemed to be the only thing keeping Erica from killing Juniper. The drive was long and quiet, and Juniper wondered if the quiet drive would become a permanent thing.

They arrived at the palace and entered the great hall to see Alice standing off to the side while Marcus paced the floor in front of her. They looked at the group, the only ones that didn't seem to be injured were Circe, Carmine, and Jason. Color hadn't completely returned to Aanya's face after being poisoned and she also had a few cuts and bruises; Zane had a bandage wrapped around his head with frost still on his face. Juniper was exhausted and Erica wasn't even walking.

"Junie, are you alright?" Marcus asked running forward to his daughter.

"I'm alright dad, I just pushed myself too far," Juniper said, "I'm more tired than hurt."

"But it seems they weren't as lucky, look at

her she's not even walking, also she's new," Alice added.

"No, she's not, she's been here before," Marcus mentioned.

"When did she show up?"

"She had a short conversation with dad, Aiden, and me. Before Aiden left she confirmed who his mother was," Juniper replied.

"Didn't you also say she wanted to kill you?" Marcus asked.

Juniper looked down, "Well yes but, we finally got to explain what really happened to her brother, so I think I'm safe."

"Are you absolutely positive? Because if you're not I will post guards outside your door tonight," Marcus whispered.

"I'll be fine dad. She can't even walk right now. Besides it's not like that would be effective she'd find another way in."

Jason stepped forward, "I trust Junie's judgment completely also, I trust Erica completely. She and Eylam were the only people I could really trust."

Carmine nodded in agreement, "She's the second highest rank and she just made an assumption out of grief, Erica's a great person."

Alice looked at them and Marcus sighed, "As much as I don't want to, I think I'll be out voted if I debate this so I'll allow her to stay but you all need to be on your best behavior my parents are visiting tomorrow, and they are the strictest people you'll ever meet." Marcus turned around and shuddered, "I'm sure to get an earful about this on top of their usual scolding and rants."

Juniper smiled and faced Erica who was still in Zane's arms, "Erica, I'm putting a great deal of faith in you," Juniper put her hand on Erica's leg, "I want you to join my side and leave the Facility behind."

"Are you sure you want to do that? You've already expended your healing quite a bit, you almost collapsed after healing me and it's only been two hours," Aanya asked.

"I'll be fine Aanya."

Juniper healed Erica's leg and as she stepped back, she fell. Carmine caught Juniper and picked her up as she lost consciousness.

Chapter 15

Juniper woke up in her room. She sat up and rubbed her eyes. She glanced to the side and saw Erica looking at her bookshelf. Erica reached up, and pulled a book off the shelf, looked over the cover then put it back. Juniper watched her walk from the bookshelf to the computer on Juniper's desk.

Erica was about to turn it on when Juniper said, "What are you doing?"

"Exploring. You were out all night, so I got bored." Erica said, studying the design of the computer, "Say what is this?"

"It's a computer, I use it to do research or keep up with the news but if I'm not home I use my phone which is a smaller version of that with more functions."

"Can it be used as a weapon?"

"It's not supposed to, but I suppose if you were desperate it could be."

"You also have a lot of books in your room, we were never allowed to have more than three checked out of the library and we had to return them in a certain amount of time."

"Yes, that tends to be how a public or school library works but all of those came from a bookstore or the private library in the palace."

Erica nodded, "This place is really different from what I'm used to." She picked up a picture from the shelf, "But what is this, it's not a book but it's here next to an abundance of them."

Juniper smiled, she thought it was funny how unfamiliar Erica was with common household items like pictures. Erica picked up a plush teddy bear that Juniper had gotten for her sixth birthday.

"This room is bigger than any room we had back home."

"Well, this isn't the Facility, this is Flora, my home kingdom." Juniper said, "It's gorgeous, isn't it?"

"Yes, it is, but why is it called Flora, I distinctly remember you bringing it up before and even then you addressed it as your home."

"The kingdom of plants, flora is another word for plant that's where the name of my kingdom came from."

"I also remember you saying something about there being five of them, what are the other four?"

"The kingdom of water, Oxidane, the

kingdom of fire, Vulcan, the kingdom of earth, Terra, and the kingdom of air, Aquilo." Juniper listed, "The royal families all have powers in accordance with their kingdoms as well."

"So, we're not supposed to have them?" Erica asked.

"Well, no when we first met, I think I said something like that, without royal blood it should be impossible to have powers much less ones that aren't anything like the royal families."

Erica rubbed her arms, she was still wearing her uniform and Juniper could see her brand, the burn was difficult to make out on Erica's dark skin, but Juniper could see the ID E06356. She also noticed that Erica had taken to carrying knives, something her brother would often do, Juniper knew for a fact that Erica preferred hand to hand over weapons.

"Erica why are you carrying knives? I thought Eylam was the knife fighter."

"He was." Erica whispered, "Until he died, so I chose to start using knives. They were his favorite after all."

Juniper looked out the window, "The knife of the back of your belt, you said that was Eylam's murder weapon, right?" She asked quietly, "Why did you keep it?"

"After you left, I picked up the blade and

sheathed it vowing to use it to kill whoever had taken the life of my brother, before I learned it wasn't you, but that wasn't the only thing I kept from him."

"What else did you keep from him?"

Erica reached into a pocket lining the inside of her jacket and pulled out a small black case. She turned around and opened it for Juniper to see inside, Juniper peered into the case and saw a pair of thick lensed black rimmed glasses.

"You took his glasses?"

"After you and Aiden ran from me and my dead brother, I took him to the infirmary," Erica said her voice quivering, "Jason was in there working, he turned and saw me put Eylam's body down on one of the beds and remove his glasses."

"What did Jason do?"

"He asked me if Eylam was okay," a tear streaked down Erica's cheek, "I said he was dead."

"Erica I'm sorry I wasn't able to save him, I was scared, and the wound was big-" Juniper said, standing up.

"Shut up, it's not your fault your powers are poorly trained, but it seems like you've gotten better with them."

"You're not still mad at me?".

"Oh, I'm furious, but not at you." Erica responded, "I saw you trying to heal his wound but instead of helping I blamed you, you didn't want him to die any more than I did, if anything I should be apologizing to you."

Juniper looked at Erica, "So can we be friends again?"

"Of course we can," Erica whispered.

The girls laughed and hugged each other. They stood for a moment before something Erica said earlier registered in Juniper's mind.

"I'm sorry but did you say I was out all night?" Juniper said, pulling away.

"Yeah, but you're fine. Jason said all you needed was rest."

"That's not the problem Erica my grandparents are visiting and if I'm not there to greet them with my parents, they'll never forgive me."

"Oh, I'm sure you'll be fine, if you explain why you overslept. They'll understand."

Juniper grabbed her phone and checked the time, she had fifteen minutes to get ready and be downstairs to greet them, "Maybe my mom's parents but these are my dad's parents, the royal side of my family, I need to be punctual and certainly can't tell them about the Facility."

"Why not?"

"Well, they're traditionalists." Juniper said, "They think a proper princess should do nothing but be regal and sip tea at dinner party, while looking nothing but perfect so if they find out about the brand and scar, they will end my father and take me to live with them at their estate."

"Oh, we wouldn't want that now, would we?" Erica said sarcastically.

"See that, that right there is the opposite of how to act around them."

Juniper changed her clothes and brushed her hair, she hopped out the door while pulling her shoes on. Juniper raced to the great hall with two minutes to spare. Her father tapped his foot impatiently and checked his watch as she ran up next to him.

"Good, you're here before they arrived but I was starting to worry you wouldn't wake up till tomorrow."

"I'm alright now, dad." Juniper said with a smile, "I feel much better now."

They smiled and waited for the old king and queen to enter the hall. They stood quietly for two more minutes when Marcus' parents walked into the hall.

"Hello Marcus, it's nice that you've finally allowed us to visit," started his mother.

"I'm sorry mother but I believe I've sent you several invitations to visit, but you never replied," Marcus replied, "I hadn't sent you one this time I just received a letter saying you were coming with very little time to prepare."

"Marcus you know that any good king is ready for an impromptu visit no matter who they are."

"Well, father things have been a tad rough lately and we were trying to put everything back to normal."

Marcus' father shook his head as his mother turned her attention to Juniper, "Juniper, look how much you've grown since we saw you last."

"Well, it has been a few years. I'm surprised you don't come by more often." Juniper said, with a bow.

"I'm also very happy to see the both of you again," Alice said.

"Oh, the feeling is mutual I'm sure Alice," the old king whispered.

Marcus sighed and Alice took his hand. Juniper brushed her hair out of her face, the old monarchs were difficult to deal with. Both Juniper and Marcus cared for them a great deal, however they needed to take several precautions to keep them happy and prevent them from forcing Marcus to do anything he didn't want to do. Queen Caroline and King Marcus the First did some incredible things during their reign so respect was a must.

"Well Mother, Father, how about joining us

in the dining hall for lunch?" Marcus asked.

"Why thank you Marcus I thought you'd never ask," his mother replied.

The couple walked out of the hall as Alice and Marcus started following them, Juniper stopped and tapped on her father's shoulder.

"I'll be a minute I need to tell my friends to stay away from the dining hall for now, or at least tell one of them and have them tell the rest." She said under her breath.

"Sounds like a good idea, I don't think my parents would like them very much."

Juniper nodded and left the hall out of a side door that led to the rooms the warriors were staying in. Juniper walked down the halls looking for one of them. Juniper turned a corner and ran into something she couldn't see.

"Carmine please don't walk around while invisible," Juniper said, brushing herself off.

"Sorry, force of habit I guess," Carmine said, and shimmered back into view, "I heard about your grandparents and thought you wouldn't want them seeing us so I elected to what I would usually do to avoid people."

"I thought you were the fourth strongest guy."

"Well, I was but you know people can't challenge what they can't see, but people also picked up on this habit and started saying 'hi

Carmine' when they walked into an empty room in case I was there."

Juniper laughed, "How often were you in there when they asked?"

"There was a one in three chance I was there, the other two was I was walking by the room, or I wasn't there." Carmine said, "I gradually did this less often after people picked up on signs I was there so there was no point in hiding. I still walked around invisible occasionally."

"Anyway, do you think you could tell the others to stay away from the dining hall for a while? Maybe stick to your rooms, the library, or the gym."

"For your grandparents?"

"Yeah."

"I will, but you might want to join them soon."

"See you later Carmine."

Juniper turned and walked down the halls to the dining hall, she opened the doors and joined her family at the table. Her grandparents seemed to have said something that upset her parents, so Juniper had to keep the peace.

"I'm terribly sorry I didn't come right away I had to take care of something."

"Well, I'm glad it didn't take up much of your time, I'd hate for anything to cause you to be able to spend less time with us," her grandfather said.

Caroline tucked her hair behind her ear, "Now what was this about there being some issues happening in the kingdom?"

"Family issues mother and they're not that big of a deal."

"Yes, as long as nothing happens then all should be fine," Alice agreed.

"So the issues weren't that big of a deal, we still want to know what they were," the old Marcus said.

"I promise you it's not that important, something happened and there are some strange things going on, but it will all be resolved soon," Juniper replied.

Juniper knew better than to tell her grandparents she had picked up fighting, especially when she wouldn't even tell her parents the full story. The old couple looked at their son who suddenly looked like he wanted to be anywhere else.

"Well, I suppose since you're so insistent that it's not a big deal we won't pry further." Caroline said, "I will say Marcus you seem to be keeping the kingdom running smoothly. It's nice to know you haven't let it fall to ruin."

The king looked at his mother, "Were you expecting me to?"

"Don't take that tone, it's unbecoming."

Juniper stifled a laugh and kept her attention on her plate. She ate while her parents and grandparents had a quiet conversation. As she listened, she wondered how to help Aiden and the other Facility members. While Juniper was lost in thought she was startled back to reality with a question from her grandfather.

"So, we heard about the engagement, and Juniper, how do you feel about the whole idea?"

"Well, when I first heard about it, I was surprised, but I'm okay with it," Juniper said, "It'll benefit the kingdoms after all."

"Well, I must say I was thrilled, after all tradition does state that the king and queen are supposed to choose the princess' husband," replied her grandfather, "Unfortunately there wasn't a similar rule about the prince's wife."

Marcus took a deep breath and looked away from his father. Alice looked at her plate and just took a bite of her food in silence.

"Anyway, how has life been at the estate?" Juniper asked.

"Oh, just as peaceful and quiet as ever," Caroline replied, "Nothing interesting is happening, just and it should be."

"Yes, if something huge happened and we didn't know about it, that would be surprising," her husband nodded in agreement.

"What would classify as surprising?" Alice questioned.

"One of you going missing," said the old Marcus.

Juniper almost choked on her drink, "Yes, something like that would be surprising."

"Yes, and I hope we'd be the first to know," Caroline said.

Juniper shifted her attention to her father, "Dad, may I speak with you for a moment."

Marcus got a nervous look, "Sure."

Alice looked at them as they walked out silently begging them not to leave her alone with her in laws. Marcus and Juniper walked out of the room into the hallway.

"Why am I so scared of my own daughter right now?" Marcus asked nervously.

"You didn't tell them that I vanished for a month?" Juniper demanded.

"I'm still alive right now so no."

"And you think they'll never find out?"

"There were very few people who knew, and they were sworn to secrecy," Marcus replied, "So no, and I'm honestly scared to know what they would do to me."

"So almost no one knew that I was gone?" Juniper asked, "For a month."

"No, after a big announcement like the engagement we didn't want to cause panic but, I was in the process of submitting a plan to reveal this information right before you got back."

"This information was never released to the public?"

"No, and I'm sorry if that makes it seem like we didn't care but I can assure you that we did everything we could to find you."

"I know dad, I just didn't expect such careful planning and low-key searches from you."

Marcus looked offended, "Wow, you expect so little of me."

"Well, you are my father."

Juniper turned and walked back into the dining hall before her father could come up with a good response.

"What was that about?" asked Alice.

"Nothing, just needed to ask him a question."

"Well Juniper, that was rather abrupt, and you seemed startled. Are you sure you're alright?" asked her grandfather.

"Oh Juniper, I've just noticed that necklace, it's awfully pretty and I don't think I've ever seen anything like it," Caroline started, "Where did you get it?"

Juniper felt the pendant as it rested on her chest, "Well a friend gave it to me, technically I earned it, but I didn't mean to. In any case it's mine now and I can't return it."

Her grandmother asked a question, but Juniper didn't hear it, she got distracted by a bright red bird outside one of the windows. The bird made eye contact with Juniper and spread its wings in front of itself as if holding a book then nodded its head before flying away.

"Juniper, are you listening to me?"

Juniper looked back at her grandmother, "Sorry I got distracted, I just need a minute I'll be right back."

Juniper stood up and walked out of the dining hall with a nervous feeling in her gut. She knew that Circe had been at the window. Why did Circe do that? Juniper walked to the library and heard voices inside and was met with quite the scene as she opened the door.

"Dang it Jason, how do you always keep winning?" Carmine growled.

"Patients always tend to downplay the pain they're feeling I've gotten really good at telling when someone is lying."

Juniper saw the group pass the cards they were holding back to Jason who began shuffling the deck.

"Playing poker I see, how much has everyone lost to Jason?"

"We weren't betting anything, but it is kinda humiliating to keep losing to someone we could easily destroy in a fight." Circe muttered.

"Listen birdy, you have your strengths I have mine."

"Is this what Circe needed me to come here to see?"

"No actually while exploring your room last night I found this envelope, they convinced me to open it." Erica said holding up a piece of paper.

"Why did you take this from my room, how did you find it?" the princess demanded.

"It wasn't well hidden first of all and I wanted to ask you about it but didn't find it till after you left to meet your grandparents."

"Why in the kingdoms did you open it?" Juniper cried.

"I was curious, and they made me do it," Erica responded pointing at the other warriors.

"Hey!" Aanya protested, "We didn't make you do anything."

"In any case I looked at the papers inside and the first one didn't make any sense, so I looked at the other one to find a picture of-"

"Don't."

"Junie, there was a whole thing written underneath the picture of him about how he died twenty years ago how is that possible."

"I promise I'll explain but if we are going to talk about him his name is Sephtis. Only ever address his as that."

"Fine but I noticed his name was also on the first piece of paper, under the term father. Upon further inspection I realized there was a name on that first sheet I recognized Kristen Blakely, someone I learned was Aiden's mother."

Juniper looked away from Erica, "I'm guessing you know what the first piece of paper was then, the word father was addressing Aiden's father."

Jason looked at Juniper, "So you're telling me that Aiden's father is-"

"Yes, that is who his father is."

The whole group was stunned, they had never expected this.

"No wonder." Zane whispered.

Aanya looked out the window, "It all makes sense now."

Circe nodded, they all heard the door to the library open, they turned to see Juniper's grandparents in the doorway stunned to see who Juniper was with while her parents stood behind them. Her father seemed disappointed, and her mother upset.

Chapter 16

The royals took in the situation. Juniper knew how it would look to them, to them it seemed like Juniper ditched them to hang out with her friends.

"What is going on here?" Marcus asked, "Juniper, did you leave to chat with them?"

Circe stepped forward, "Your Majesty I promise I didn't ask her to join us in the library without reason."

"First question, how did you ask her to join you? I feel we would have remembered a girl with pink hair coming in and talking to the princess. Secondly, what exactly was the reason you needed to speak with her at all?" the old Marcus questioned.

"Second question first, family matters of a friend. As for the first question well-" Aanya started.

Juniper stomped on her foot to shut her up, "They have their ways to get my attention."

Alice stepped past her in-laws, "Who is this

friend and what family matters?"

Juniper couldn't meet her parents' gaze, "Aiden's father." She murmured softly.

"I'm sorry, what was that?" Alice responded.

"We were asking about Aiden's father, and we learned who he was." Carmine explained.

"Considering who his mother is, it wouldn't have mattered he's probably dead." Alice replied.

"Oh yeah according to internet searches and Vulcan law he has been dead for twenty years, the funny part is Aiden is nineteen." Juniper said.

The royals looked stunned, and Circe looked at them with a smug smile, "Told you it was important."

"Circe stop the sarcasm, but here's when this gets really interesting."

Juniper held up the envelope, "July thirtieth, twenty years ago Sephtis Kai, Aiden's father was found dead in his home with the same MO and calling card from Rare Ruby before her identity was revealed. Upon further investigation of this man, I can infer he was legally married to Kristen who didn't take his last name before faking his death meaning Aiden's last name is hyphenated, but that's not important."

"Hate to disagree with you Junie but it has been twenty-one years since his death, today is July thirtieth." Marcus said.

Jason looked at Juniper wide eyed, "Wait a minute, today is July thirtieth?"

Juniper looked over her shoulder at him, "Apparently."

"Well first of all Sephtis faked his death exactly a year before his son was born and today is Aiden's birthday, he's twenty now."

"Okay well good for him. Happy birthday to Aiden and his father faked his death exactly a year before his son's birth, what ironic and perfect timing."

"Marcus, who are they talking about?" Caroline asked.

"I'm assuming myself," replied a voice from atop the bookshelves.

Juniper looked up at the man on the shelves, "Where do you keep coming from? I thought you said leaving would make him more angry at you."

"While he has been stricter with me, he can't stop me from casually breaking the rules."

Juniper glared at him, "Well I must say, happy birthday... king."

"No."

Aiden jumped to the floor in front of them, he wasn't wearing the usual uniform anymore, he had a black two piece suit on with a simple white button up. He had two knives one strapped to his left leg the other on his upper arm, his pendant was visible resting on the knot of his tie. There was a pistol on his hip, with one of the Commander's roses worn on the lapel of his jacket.

"If he's being so strict how exactly can you 'casually' break rules?" Jason asked.

Juniper looked Aiden up and down, "Nice outfit by the way."

"Just don't even, anyway a new tracker was never placed on me, and he's been spending almost all of his time in his study only ever leaving to get food. I'm pretty much free to do whatever I want as long as I don't get caught."

Erica nodded, "And what's likelihood of that happening."

"Lower than you'd think."

Jason stepped forward, "Junie pointed it out already, but I have to ask, what with the clothes?"

"Commander came into my room this morning dropped this outfit on my bed and said it was my new uniform."

Juniper's grandparents pulled her behind them, "Who's he?" demanded her grandfather.

Caroline sized him up, "At least he's dressed appropriately, unlike them."

The others were still wearing their uniforms, except for Jason, "I'm genuinely surprised they still haven't changed out of those clothes."

"I'm sorry do we have anything to change into?" Aanya muttered.

Juniper rolled her eyes, "Anyway grandmother, grandfather, that is the one whose father we were talking about earlier, Aiden Blakely-Kai."

"I'm sorry, what's this about my father and did you just say Blakely-Kai?"

"Aiden, your father's name is Sephtis Kai, I tried to tell you about him yesterday, but you left before I could." Juniper replied.

"W-what did you find out about him? Is he alive in one of the kingdoms? Could I see him?" Aiden begged, starting to get a little freaked out.

Juniper looked at the floor and stepped around her grandparents. She walked over to the table where the envelope was sitting and picked it up. Juniper held up the envelope in front of Aiden, "Everything you need to know about him is here. Promise me you won't let the Commander find out you have this. If he knew we'd all be killed."

Aiden took the envelope, "Why? What's in here?"

"Look at it when you get back, but please believe me when I say the Commander would never want you to know what's in here. He kept your parents from you for a reason Aiden."

Aiden nodded and tucked the envelope away

in his jacket, "So Princess, how's royal life been? Anything interesting?"

"Not really, but shouldn't you be getting back soon instead of increasing your risk of getting caught by chatting?" Juniper said sarcastically.

"Oh princesses and their need to be right."

"Firstly sexist, secondly answer truthfully, am I wrong?"

Aiden glared at Juniper then looked away, "Okay but there's one more thing I need to say."

Juniper looked up at him, "What?"

"When the Commander gave me this new wardrobe and dress code, he told me that" Aiden's voice caught, "That I..." he trailed off.

"You what?" Erica asked.

The group looked at Aiden, he turned away, and shook his head, "Never mind it's not important." he took a shaky breath, "I should go, before a guard makes rounds to make sure I'm still behaving properly they come by more often."

Aiden turned and jumped onto one of the windowsills, but Juniper wrapped vines around his legs locking him in place, "Wait, that sounded important."

Aiden didn't turn back, "Let me go, I'll see you soon I promise."

"You make an awful lot of promises," Juniper said, "I hope you intend to keep them."

The vines on Aiden slacked and fell away, his hands sparked, and he vanished in a puff of fire. The royals looked at where Aiden just stood in surprise, when Juniper remembered that pyroportation, while being a fire power was not one of the Vulcan royal family.

Juniper turned to her family, "Pyroportation."

Alice looked confused, "What?"

"That's what Aiden just did teleportation through fire, in order for that to work I'm assuming he set up a pre-existing fire to return to so he could go to and from without raising alarms."

"I wonder what he wanted to say," Carmine whispered, "He seemed scared by it, so it must've been bad. Aiden doesn't scare easily."

Marcus I looked at Carmine, "When you say he doesn't scare easily what do you-"

"Aiden could be backed into a wall by five serial killers nobody has ever seen and lived to tell the tale, cut off from his powers with no weapons and still not be intimidated."

"He'd also win that fight in no more than five minutes," continued Circe, "He is truly a force to be reckoned with."

"I'm sorry Juniper but how exactly did you meet these people? I'm not sure I approve of them hanging around," Caroline asked.

Juniper looked at the warriors, unsure of how to answer in a way that would sound good. She went through a few different reasons in head when her father answered for her.

"They're the children of a few guards here they are currently training to join their ranks, and they should return to their rooms for the time being."

The warriors looked at each other before nodding their heads in agreement and shuffling out of the room. Juniper's grandparents looked at the table the warriors had been sitting at.

"What were they doing in here?" questioned Marcus I.

"They had a free day, so they were hanging out, they decided to play poker but weren't betting anything because they had nothing to bet but Jason was winning every set." Juniper answered.

"Alright then, Marcus can we speak with you privately?" asked his father.

"Of course," Marcus replied.

The trio walked away, and Juniper faced her mother, "I'm going to get the others some new clothes to wear they can't stay in those uniforms."

"Yeah, you probably should."

Juniper left the library and walked down the halls to the warriors' rooms. As she walked her mind wandered to all the questions she had about the Commander and his Facility. Where was this huge place located? Why hadn't anyone found or come across it, even by accident? How did all these people get their powers? Why did the Commander choose the rose as his symbol? Why had he chosen to kill Eylam? As soon as that thought came to her mind she stopped in the middle of the hall.

"I don't have time for this," Juniper muttered.

She did her best to push the depressing thoughts of Eylam and his death away. She didn't have the time to mourn or grieve. With everything going on around her she needed to move forward and protect her home.

"First things first Juniper, you need to finish all the wedding planning, rescue Aiden, help all the others get freedom, then you can stop and breathe." She said to herself. Upon the wedding coming to her mind she hesitated, "Do I really want to go through with that?" Juniper thought about all that's already happened, "No don't think like that. Your parents want you to go through with this. It's the best option I can't let them down."

"Let who down?" asked a voice next to her.

Juniper jumped and saw Circe leaning in her doorway smirking, "How much of that did you hear?"

"Just that last part about not wanting to disappoint people."

"It's rude to eavesdrop."

"It's hard not to when your friend is thinking out loud in front of the room she loans to you." Circe teased.

Juniper rolled her eyes and walked into the room, she didn't notice anything major in the room aside from the bow and quiver of arrows leaning against the desk. The room itself was relatively plain as far as palace bedrooms go, it had a big bed, a bookshelf, a desk, a full bathroom, and a huge closet. There were a few potted plants and a balcony with vines lining the rail. All the guest rooms were pretty uniform, so the others were living in the same thing which is to say quite a step up from facility rooms.

"So why exactly were you standing outside my room?" Circe asked.

"I was going to help all of you get some better clothes and get you out of those uniforms."

Circe shrugged and gestured toward the closet, "I already would have but I wasn't sure what I was allowed to touch or move."

"It's fine if you make a mess or move things. It's your room, you pretty much have free reign, just don't break anything and try to be respectful of the cleaning staff," Juniper assured her while walking into the closet.

Juniper went through the clothing already in the closet and found a pretty outfit she thought Circe would like and would fit.

"Here, try this on you can change in either the closet or bathroom then bring your uniform to me I want to do something to them."

"Alright, but what if these clothes don't fit?"

"Then go through the closet for some that do."

Juniper left and went to the other rooms, with the same routine of getting a new outfit for them and telling them to put their old uniforms in her room. She never saw anything too unusual, other than hearing Carmine lightly strumming a guitar he said he found in the music room and promised to return. She was stunned by how cold Zane liked his room. Juniper liked her room a little more on the chilly side but not like how Zane did.

She stopped by Jason's room before heading back to her parents, "Hey Jason, do you still have your uniform?" Juniper asked from one side of the door.

Jason opened the door and faced her, "You couldn't have knocked, or you know, just come in?"

"Do you still have it or not?"

"Yeah, hang on."

"No just fold it up and put it in my room I'm gathering everyone's."

Jason nodded and Juniper stopped in her room. She walked over to her nightstand and pushed it out from the wall to access the secret compartment in the back. She opened the door and pulled out a uniform.

"Why did I keep this, it's not even mine?" Juniper muttered under her breath as she pushed the nightstand back against the wall.

She set the uniform down on her desk and walked down to the throne room. As she opened the door, she saw her grandparents leave via a door on the other side of the hall. As soon as the door closed Marcus rubbed his temples with an exasperated sigh.

"What am I going to do?" he said.

Juniper was about to enter the room when a guard walked in the main entrance and knelt at the foot of the throne, "Pardon me my liege, but your three o'clock is here."

Juniper quietly closed the door and walked back to her room deciding against talking to her father. She opened the door to her room and saw her balcony door was open.

"I didn't open that when I came by a few minutes ago," Juniper said confused.

She looked around and saw the others had put their uniforms next to the one she left on her desk. Juniper shut the balcony doors and heard rummaging in her closet. Juniper took off her shoes so as not to spook whoever was in her closet. She inched her way forward and pushed the door open as quietly as possible. As soon as Juniper looked inside Melanie walked out.

"Oh, I'm sorry Your Highness."

"What were you doing in my closet?"

Melanie looked down, "I was organizing, did you think I was someone else?"

"Ah, never mind Melanie, I saw the balcony door open, and I hadn't opened it so you scared me." Juniper admitted.

"Well, my apologies, Princess it was just a tad stuffy in here, so I opened them to let fresh air in. I'm finished with my work, so I'll be taking my leave now." Melanie said as she walked toward the door, "Unless you need anything?"

"No, I'm alright thank you though."

Melanie left the room and Juniper flopped down on her bed. She took her phone from her pocket, she held up the small screen and searched for more information about the families of Kristen Blakely and Sephtis Kai. While searching around she learned that Kristen's parents and siblings were still alive as were Sephtis' as well as his younger brother Samuel.

"Aiden has living relatives that might accept him." Juniper thought aloud, "Wish I'd known that sooner."

Juniper looked for more information about Samuel Kai, and learned more about his family and career. He works for a semiconductor company and has a stay-at-home wife with his two kids, Estelle and Carter.

"Should I set out to find them?" Juniper pondered, "Would my father even let me? He seems to be losing trust in me. Each passing hour I don't tell him more," She shook her head, "I'll find and speak with them soon for now I need to complete the task at hand."

Juniper stood up and examined the clothing on her desk, once she deciphered and labeled what belonged to each one, she walked down the armory with clothing measurements in hand.

Chapter 17

Juniper left the armory thirty minutes later holding what she needed. She dropped her supplies in her room and walked down to the basement where the servants' quarters were. She retrieved a group of different fabrics and threads then returned to her room with everything she needed and set to work remaking the uniforms.

"A single outfit shouldn't take more than a couple hours. I already have a base. I just need to re-cut all of the pieces on separate fabric," Juniper muttered as she worked with a seam ripper.

She cut through the seams and traced the pieces of clothing on paper and began cutting fabric. She worked with a sewing machine to stitch together clothing with the color schemes of the five kingdom's flags while also making them match the owner.

Juniper worked for hours and managed to complete four sets before she looked outside to see the sun had set and the stars shining in the sky. Juniper looked at the clock on the wall to see that it was eleven o'clock at night.

"How did the time pass so quickly? Nobody even came to tell me dinner was ready."

Juniper wracked her brain to remember if anyone had entered her room during the day, as she thought long and hard, she realized how exhausted she was. Juniper walked into her bathroom to change and wash her face. The princess walked over to her bed and collapsed onto it.

As she started to dream, she saw Aiden sitting at a desk in his room back at the Facility. He was going over some papers with a golden crown embedded with rubies designed for a prince sitting in a case on a shelf. Juniper watched as he looked over at the crown and glared at it.

"I hate you," he muttered.

Juniper looked around, "Why am I seeing this, by all means nobody I know has a power like this."

Suddenly the room echoed around her then began to speak in a voice she didn't recognize, "Nobody as far as you know princess, but I know of a person who can do this."

"Who are you?" Juniper shouted.

"Please lower your voice princess, you need to see this. But do try and remember that in the mind, time is relative, what may only seem like a mere minutes to you could be hours for others."

"Are you the one holding me here," Juniper questioned.

"Indeed, I am," the voice jeered, "Aiden can't hear you by the way. Try as you might to reach him he'll never know you were here."

Juniper looked back at Aiden, he had dark circles under his eyes. Juniper knew those hadn't been there when he came by the palace earlier. Aiden rubbed his eyes and leaned back in his chair.

"I need to finish this before he comes back, especially since he's now forbidden me from leaving this room without someone with me at all times."

There was a knock at the door, but whoever was knocking didn't wait for a reply and just walked in.

"I see you still haven't finished your work." said the Commander, "Honestly Aiden I expect more from you."

"You gave me two days' worth of things to get done in only a few hours."

"And by your level of productivity and how I raised you, you should have completed it with time to spare, but alas you failed."

Aiden continued going over the papers, "Why do you have so many people watching me all of a sudden."

The Commander looked at Aiden sourly, "Fix you posture you're slouching," he ordered, "Also I know about your little visit to Flora earlier today, and now you will always have someone with you, I will know if you leave no matter how."

"Can I at least have my room completely to myself?"

The Commander shook his head, "No, because of those little stunts you pulled you have completely lost my trust and your little bit of freedom within these walls."

He walked over to Aiden and placed a hand on his shoulder, "I've lost too many good warriors to risk losing my strongest. You understand, don't you?"

Aiden glanced at the hand on his shoulder, "Yeah, now I'm going to finish this. I'm just about done anyway."

"Good. Leave them in my office when you're finished then go to bed. You have more work in the morning." The Commander turned to leave, "Oh, and Aiden don't make me regret choosing you as my heir."

Aiden nodded and the Commander left, "I wish I could do anything you approved of, but I'll never be good enough." He removed an envelope from his pocket, "I just don't get it, this made everything worse, all these lies."

Juniper shot up in bed, light flooding through the windows.

"Aiden is the Commander's heir?" Juniper shouted, her head fell into her hands, "No no no no no no, why does that make perfect sense?"

The door to her room opened and her grandmother, Caroline, entered the room, "Good morning, Juniper, it's a pity you didn't join us for dinner last night." She looked at the clothes on her desk, "It also seems as though you had a rough night considering you woke up shouting something I couldn't quite hear."

"Sorry, I was busy and lost track of time."

"Yes, it seems you were," Caroline walked over and sat on the edge of the bed, "Juniper are you alright, because if you're not I swear Marcus will-"

"No, I'm fine." Juniper said quickly, "Even if something happened then my parents would be there to help, they wouldn't be making it worse."

"Well, if you're absolutely sure then I'll believe you."

"But if you don't mind, I should finish my work."

Caroline sighed, "Alright but we're leaving tomorrow and if you have anything to say we're always available."

Caroline left the room while Juniper went back to her project after getting dressed. She toiled away with fabric and armor while making sure weapons and powers were accommodated for. After a few hours Juniper had completed yet another set when there was a knock on the door.

"Who is it?" called Juniper, continuing with the next outfit.

"Me," responded a voice, "Long time no see, friend."

"Hi Silvia," Juniper said, turning around, "How's your family been?"

"Same as always, but have you seen Tracker? He got spooked and ran off."

"No, I haven't, I haven't left my room today, so a better question would be when did you get here and why?"

"It's the annual meeting where our parents talk and we get the afternoon to hang out. My family was the first here."

"So did you come here first, or did you check the library beforehand?"

Silvia thought for a moment, "I was told you were here, but Diana went to the library to look for Tracker. Could you help us find my mom's seeing eye dog?"

Juniper looked back at her work, "I suppose I'm not too busy to help out a friend."

Juniper and Silvia left and started down the halls in search of the missing dog, they walked through the palace calling for Tracker for a while before Silvia finally asked a question,

"Why did you skip out on hanging out with us? We never did get an answer." Silvia asked.

Juniper froze, "I don't really want to get into it."

"We all were really looking forward to meeting this guy you showed up with, you said is name was-"

"Please don't talk about him."

"Why!? What happened?"

"Nothing Silvia I promise, so please stop prying."

Silvia looked hurt by what Juniper had said when there was a shout from down the hall. The young princesses took off down the hall and when they turned a corner, they saw Jason backed up against a wall with a dog sniffing his hands and feet.

"Junie, help me!" Jason begged.

"Jason, are you okay?"

Silvia was giggling, and Jason scowled at her, "Just get this away from me."

Silvia calmed down and took a deep breath, "Tracker, heel."

The dog obediently turned away and stood

calmly by Silvia while Jason inched along the wall past the dog then returned to his room.

"Who was that?" Silvia asked, turning down the halls motioning for the dog to follow.

"That was Jason, one of the other people I met."

"I thought only one returned with you."

"Yes, that's true but circumstances changed and now a larger group is staying here."

The two girls entered the throne room to return Tracker to the queen of Oxidane. Silvia walked to a woman with similar golden blonde hair and guided her hand to the dog's harness. Slowly the queen let go of her husband's arm.

"There you go, mom," Silvia said quietly.

"Thank you, Silvia."

The king looked over his shoulder and pushed his glasses up his nose, "Juniper, glad to see you're alright from your month away."

"Thank you, Your Majesty. It's also nice you see you're well."

"I have been curious, princess, what happened to you during that month?" the king asked.

"Nothing of consequence King David. Queen Julia I'm glad we were able to find Tracker."

"As am I."

David pushed his light brown hair away from his eyes, "You should go tell Diana that Tracker was found."

The princesses nodded and left the throne room to see the royal family of Vulcan about to enter the room.

"Queen Lacy, King Timothy, how are you?" Juniper said quickly.

"We're quite alright thank you, Juniper, but I'm more concerned about you," Lacy replied.

"Whatever do you mean Your Majesty?" Juniper asked.

Timothy shrugged, "You went missing then showed up out of nowhere. We were worried you were hurt."

"Well as you can see, I'm perfectly fine."

Victoria looked at her father, "Now if you don't mind, we'd like to go hang out for a while."

Victoria turned to leave when her mother stopped her, "Victoria take your brothers."

Victoria sighed, "Come on you two." The group walked down the hall until they were out of earshot of Victoria's parents, "Damian, Lucas, if you two cause any sort of trouble I will end you. Juniper was gone for a month, and I want time alone with my friend."

The boys looked at each other with disappointed looks then followed the girls silently to the library. They strolled silently when there was a call for their attention behind them.

"We saw you walk away but didn't want to call out for you cause..." An out of breath prince managed.

"Aeolus, are you okay?" Elaine asked from behind him.

"It wasn't that long a walk, are you dying?" Silvia questioned.

"Oh, shut up" Aeolus muttered.

Victoria was trying hard not to laugh, "That's no way for a crown prince to act, Your Highness."

"Are we seriously doing this today?" Aeolus said, regaining his composure.

"Hey, do you know who this guy is? I found him in the library." said a voice from behind the group.

A young princess with light brown hair and blue eyes the spitting image of her father walked forward with a swordsmith in tow.

"Diana, the man you have there is Carmine, he's a friend of mine." Juniper replied, "If you could be so kind as to let him go?"

Diana shrugged and released Carmine's wrist who immediately walked behind Juniper, "Junie who are these people?" Carmine whispered.

"The other royals." Juniper whispered back, she turned toward the group and saw someone else walking down the halls, "Oh and there's Hazel! Carmine be respectful."

Carmine looked down, "Why exactly? They don't look all that strong or powerful I could easily best them in a fight."

The royals gave Carmine and Juniper strange looks, she smiled quickly and pushed Carmine down the hall out of earshot of the group.

"I thought I explained that things work differently here, while what you said is most likely true, you'd be arrested for fighting them. It has to do less with strength and more with blood." Juniper explained, "They will always outrank you because they're royalty and you need get over it."

Carmine nodded his head and walked away while Juniper returned to her friends.

"What was that about?" Hazel asked.

"Also, who was that?" Damian chimed in.

"That was Carmine, I already said that. But he's used to life running differently he doesn't quite understand how life here works quite yet."

"Okay... Well anyway what should we do while we're here?" Aeolus asked.

"Yeah, it's not often we're all in the same place that's not a formal gala or something," Elaine added.

Silvia looked at Juniper, "Junie was making clothes when I saw her in her room earlier. Could we get a closer look at what you were making?"

"I suppose I could show you what I'm making. If you really wanted to see it."

"You were making clothes?" Victoria asked.

"Well, I already had bases I just needed to trace them on new fabric and make some small adjustments."

"Well, I for one would love to see what you've created," Aeolus said.

"Oh of course you would Aeolus," Silvia retorted.

"Whatever is that supposed to mean?" he asked, rather angered by the comment.

"Oh nothing," Diana said with a smile, "Nothing at all."

Juniper turned and walked down the halls and the group followed her to her room. She walked to her desk and picked up a clothing set. She handed it to Elaine who unfolded it and looked it over. She was holding a dark green jacket draped over a light purple shirt with armored sleeves that allowed the hands to always be completely visible. The pants were padded to protect the joints while not restricting movement, they were light gray and had hidden slits for hiding knives and other small weapons.

"That one if for my friend Erica, while this one-" Juniper said picking up another set, "-Is for Carmine."

Diana picked up the outfit, the fabric was light and breathable for quick movement with a layer of bulletproof fabric stitched into the light green shirt, and light brown jacket padding the arms fitted closely to not drift too far from the bodice. There was a mask the same color as the jacket to cover the sound of breathing. Tucked into the pockets of the bottoms were a pair of leather gloves meant to protect the hands while sword fighting.

Hazel looked at the clothes, "They seem to be modeled after the flags of Flora and Terra."

"Also, they seem to be made for combat." Victoria noted.

"Well, yes, their color scheme was designed after the flags of their home kingdom as we met their parents recently while also maintaining parts of how they look, the purple on Erica's and the green of Carmine's it goes with their eyes."

"Okay but why are they designed for combat?" Aeolus asked.

"They are fighters and needed new clothes," Juniper said, "Some that better suited who they are."

"So, who's this one for?" Victoria asked, holding up a new set.

It included a white shirt with a pastel green cover made from a sturdy fabric. The short sleeves had padding on the shoulders and light flexible bottoms with a belt that provided protection of the lower half of the body. The belt had a spot for a sword sheath and spots for hidden knives. Fabric the colors of the Flora flag with spots of white.

Juniper looked away, "I suppose I got caught up in working with this fabric and made one for myself."

"Why in the five kingdoms would you need fighting gear?" Diana asked.

"Well, I don't intend to use it!" Juniper assured them, "It was just fun to make."

Lucas inched past the group with his brother hiding something behind his back. Victoria looked over her shoulder to see them, "Where are you two going?"

"Nowhere," Damian muttered.

Victoria didn't look convinced, "What's Lucas hiding behind his back?"

Aeolus slid around behind the boys and took what Lucas was holding, to look at it, "Is this a knife?"

Juniper rushed forward and took it from Aeolus, "Sorry." She turned and looked at the blade, "Please don't ask questions about where I got this."

"Juniper there was blood on that hilt, I can

only imagine what that blade looks like."

She looked down and saw the stains of dark red covering the hilt, "It's nothing, Aeolus, I said not to ask questions."

Elaine looked concerned, "Junie, we know you've been keeping secrets. Something is wrong."

"No, it's not."

"Yes, it is. I can see it clear as day you're not okay," Silvia said, nearly shouting.

"I'm fine, nothing has happened," Juniper argued.

Aeolus grabbed Juniper's arm, "Why are you still lying?"

"I said I'm still fine!" Juniper shouted, the group was stunned, "Pardon my volume."

Juniper pushed past the group and left the room holding the blade close to her chest. If there was one thing Juniper never did, it was raise her voice, people could always tell what she was feeling. She heard Diana call out to her, however Juniper ignored her and walked down to Erica's room. Juniper entered the room without knocking or a word.

"Junie, are you okay." Erica asked quickly.

Juniper shook her head while her friend stood up and embraced her, "Erica I'm sorry."

"Sorry for what?"

Juniper wiped her face, "Losing your brother, nearly getting myself killed, letting Aiden break your leg-"

"Woah calm down you've already done this, it's okay I've forgiven you," Erica muttered calmly.

"You and the others are the only people I can discuss what happened with. You went through it too but it's getting far more difficult to push these feelings away."

"Juniper, repressing how you feel is never going to help matters."

"I have to Erica, if I continue to think about these things, if I continue to feel these things..." Juniper trailed off.

"You're avoiding something." Erica whispered, "Do you want to talk about it."

"No because if i say it out loud then it becomes true."

"Do you not want it to be?"

Tears continued falling from Juniper's eyes, "I don't know, I'm scared Erica. The Commander is still after us, whether it's to gain us back as allies or to have us killed for leaving."

"You need to calm down and relax. First, are you scared to tell your family about these thoughts?"

Juniper nodded, "If I tell them they'll be

disappointed in me."

Erica was taken aback, "In the very short time I've met your family, I've seen nothing but kindness and caring from your parents. You should have seen the way your father freaked out when you collapsed after healing my leg and the murderous look he gave Carmine as he took you to your room."

"Oh, I'm sure."

"Maybe because of how scared you are to tell them whatever it is you've been thinking about, you should be telling them."

Juniper was about to say something when there was a gentle knock on the door, "Who is it?"

Melanie opened the door, "Your Highness your presence is requested in the throne room."

"While they're in a meeting?"

"I don't question what His Majesty requests, Princess I simply do as he asks."

Juniper stood up, "Well we wouldn't want to keep them all waiting."

Melanie bowed her head as Juniper walked past. She walked quietly through the halls and entered the room. As she walked in, she noticed Aeolus waiting off to the side, Juniper kept her focus on her father who waved his hand for her to stand by the prince.

"So, we decided rather than wait we think it

best to have the two of you get married as soon as possible," Marcus stated.

Juniper and Aeolus looked at each other, "How soon would that be?" Juniper asked.

"The second, this coming Sunday." Marcus answered.

"That gives us only two days to prepare not counting today, Your Majesty."

"Yes Aeolus." Jacqueline started, "We thought it best after all that's happened that we make sure there is no time for anything else."

"How exactly are you ensuring that nothing else will happen? Two days can prove to be a long time."

"Princess, are you asking we push it back or bring it forward?" Malachi asked.

"Oh no, the date set if fine, I'm only trying to say a lot can happen in the shortest amount of time," Juniper said quietly, "I'm greatly looking forward to it. Now if you'll excuse me."

Juniper turned and left for her room. As she entered the other royals asked if she was alright.

"If you all don't mind, I'd like to be alone." The royals left the room as Juniper requested. Juniper rubbed her arms and sat down on her bed and looked out the window, "I don't want this."

Just as Juniper told Erica once she said it, she knew it was true.

Chapter 18

Juniper spent the rest of the day in her room finishing the clothes for her friends. It was around seven when she had completed them all. Every set was fitted with armor to protect joints and vital organs, while remaining adaptable to what each person needed, Zane's being nice and warm lined with flannel and fur while Jason's had pouches for anything he needed to carry.

Juniper was silently folding the clothes to put away when her door opened, "Hey Juniper."

"Erica, what are you doing in here? I figured you would be getting dinner."

"Thought you were more important." Erica looked at Juniper, "Are you alright?"

Juniper took a quivering breath, "No."

"What's wrong?"

Tears welled up in Juniper's eyes, "I don't want this, I don't want to marry Aeolus."

"So, say something, tell someone, tell your parents."

"I can't"

"Why not?"

"I just can't, if I did, they'd be disappointed in me," she sputtered out between sobs.

"You can't truly believe that your parents would be disappointed in you for that can you?"

"My parents want me to marry Aeolus, his parents want me to marry Aeolus, even my grandparents want me to marry Aeolus. So why don't I?"

"Only you would know how you truly feel about someone." Erica said to her friend, "By the way I have to know what you were working on in here?"

Juniper picked up the outfit she made for Erica, "I made you all new personalized fighting clothes, there are slits in the pants for hidden knives."

Erica looked over the new clothes, "Sweet, did you say you made a set for everyone?"

"Yeah, I was in here finishing them to help keep my mind off of Aeolus and the wedding." Juniper said, wiping the tears from her face, "They're all designed to be better suited for your powers as well, Carmine's to stay close to his body, and Zane's to keep him warm."

"That's really cool Junie."

Juniper nodded, "Yeah but honestly I just want to be alone."

"Junie if you don't want to go through with this, I'll tell your parents for you if I have to."

Juniper shook her head, "That is a nice thought but no, I must do what's expected of me," she paused, "And I'm expected to marry Aeolus so that's what I'm going to do."

Erica nodded, "Okay if you want to go through with something that doesn't make you happy then I won't stop you it's your choice."

The warrior left, leaving Juniper alone. The next two days consisted of nothing but rapid wedding preparations. Over the next forty-eight hours Juniper and Aeolus were hardly ever apart, making decisions about everything. Newscasters and paparazzi followed them everywhere they went. Everyone wanted photos and interviews with the soon to be married royal couple.

The night before the wedding Juniper was dragged back into another dream watching Aiden work.

"So, as you know it's almost time," the Commander said.

Aiden looked exhausted, "Why exactly are we starting this tomorrow?"

"Because tomorrow all the royal families are in the same place as well as noble and wealthy like Zane's family."

"Why are you targeting them?"

"Those escaped warriors need to be taught a lesson so their families will be taken care of." The Commander stepped toward Aiden, "And I'll finally have her back. All you need to do is keep them all in line until I can get them to sign over the kingdoms to me."

Aiden left the office while the Commander looked right at Juniper.

"You. This is your doing. Your powers are keeping me here," Juniper said angrily.

"Well princess you certainly figured that out fast, yes, my powers relate to the mind. Most theories were close but never quite on the mark."

"Don't come near the wedding tomorrow."

"I thought that crashing it would be amazing for you because you don't want this. Also, I'm giving you a warning."

Juniper woke up the next morning with maids in her room waiting to get her ready for the big day. Juniper and Aeolus along with their families had stayed in rooms at the venue of the wedding. Juniper steadied her breathing.

"You're okay it was just a dream; it's not really going to happen."

One of the maids stepped forward, "Are you alright, Your Highness?"

"Perfectly well thank you."

"Well then, we should begin getting you ready.

Are you excited?"

"Yes, it was difficult to get to sleep last night because of nerves."

The maids giggled and began helping Juniper get ready. The next few hours consisted of getting Juniper's makeup, hair, and nails done. After all that was complete, the staff helped her get her dress and shoes on. Juniper looked at her reflection in the mirror, her sandy blonde hair pulled in a half up half down style with flowers, with a simple floor length gown with a halter top showing none of her back to keep the scar and brand hidden from the eyes of everyone, and long white gloves.

"Princess, you look stunning." one of the maids whispered, "Also you have someone who wants to see you before the wedding."

"Who?"

"Why your parents of course."

Juniper nodded, "Okay."

"Your Highness, are you feeling alright?"

"I'm feeling perfectly well, just pre-wedding nerves I suppose."

The maid nodded and opened the door for her parents who stopped when they saw her.

"Junie, look at you," Alice said.

Juniper smiled while Marcus placed a hand on her shoulder, "You grew up way too fast."

"Wasn't this your idea, dad?"

"Yes."

Juniper stifled a laugh and turned her attention back to her reflection with a frown that her mother noticed, "Junie are you alright, you look upset."

"I'm alright mom, I promise. I just had a restless night."

Marcus wasn't convinced, "Are you sure, you're looking rather pale?"

"I'm fine, dad." Juniper faked a smile, "See, just nervous is all. Weren't you on your wedding day?"

"That's a fantastic point Juniper, but I'm going to get our seats while Marcus will wait at the back for you," Alice said, "See you soon."

The king and queen walked out of the room, leaving Juniper looking at her reflection once again. She looked at the clock then turned to leave so the ceremony could start when she heard glass shattering and loud screams. Juniper immediately closed and locked the door grabbing a hidden bag she put her fighting clothes in.

Juniper took off her dress as quickly as she could changing into the fighting clothes and had to decide she didn't have the time to remove makeup in favor of removing her corset. She pulled combat boots on and opened a window holding her hand straight out and focusing on her sword. After several minutes the sheathed blade was in her hand along with twin daggers tied to the sword. She attached the weapons to her belt and climbed out the window and made her way to the room she asked the warriors to stay in during the wedding.

"Don't do this Vivian," Carmine said sternly to a girl standing against the wall holding a gun to Jason's head.

"Don't come a step closer or I will kill the healer," Vivian growled.

Jason pulled against her grip, "Vivian please, I healed you. You were nearly killed, if it weren't for me, you'd be dead right now."

"Like I care. You may have saved my life but you're still worthless and weak."

When the young warrior said that, something inside Jason snapped. He lifted his arm and drove his elbow into her gut, then kicked her nose as hard as he could.

"I'm not worthless nor am I weak, I chose to appear that way, and chose to not climb the ranks and be picked on and beaten by all of you for years so you wouldn't be scared of me," Jason shouted, "It's difficult to help people who won't look you in the eye."

Juniper ran past them and bound her hands

and wrists with vines then gagging her with another, "Wow Jason, I didn't know you could do that."

"I was always good at fighting; I just didn't want to show it off."

Juniper shrugged, "Did all of you bring that new fighting gear I made you?"

Aanya tilted her head, "Yeah, why?"

"Really, you're asking why? Jason was almost killed by a Facility member! The Commander brought more, change and follow me."

They all went to separate corners and changed into their new fighting clothes, Aanya turned around wearing a light gray top with purplish bands protecting her arms with a perfectly fitted chest plate over top, her holsters were fitted perfectly over top as well, her shorts while not protecting her legs allowed for any judo move she wanted to perform. Circe then joined the group with a red leather cover on a white shirt, steel shoulder guards and finger covers for her bow, her pants with a spot for her matches and boots that were easy to run in. Her bow and quiver slung neatly on her back with a scope on her arm for better aim.

Zane was wearing light fall attire in winter colors, ice boots lined with fur to keep him warm and help prevent slipping, shoulder and elbow pads to continue supplying warmth and protection, while not restricting movement so he could skate freely on his ice to dodge attacks. Jason was the last to join the group with green camouflage over a bulletproof vest, and padding on his arms and legs, there were pouches on the camouflage shirt and attached to his belt for first aid kits as well at scalpels and syringes with medicine just in case someone needed more advanced healing.

"Never tried these on before now Juniper, these are great." Carmine exclaimed.

"Yeah, you managed to get them perfectly matched with our powers and skill set." Circe added.

"Take time to admire the handy work later, right now focus on saving my family and friends."

"Right, that's a better plan." Carmine said.

Juniper nodded and led them down the halls to a space where they could watch the event hall where everything was currently happening. Juniper peered into the room to see Aeolus, Diana, Victoria, and Hazel forcefully dragged out of the room while the checkered rose support group was being chained to the wall along with a man, two women, and a couple of children Juniper didn't recognize.

Aiden was standing at the front of the hall

with his hands tucked into his pockets and the crown Juniper saw in his room attached to his hip, "So now that you've got them all here what's your plan?" he asked, "You said you wanted to get them to sign their kingdoms over but how does that work exactly?"

The Commander looked over at him, "I don't think that is any of your concern, boy."

Aiden looked at the ground, when Alexi the King of Terra spoke up, "What have you done with our children?"

"You would do well to remain quiet unless you have been addressed, Your Majesty."

Juniper heard a dog barking and snarling at the Commander. He scowled at the dog before turning away. The dog lunged forward at the Commander, teeth bared, Juniper realized it was Tracker, the blind Queen Julia's seeing eye dog. The Commander pivoted on his heel brandishing a knife slitting the poor dog's throat. Juniper heard the entire room gasp; the Commander snapped his fingers and pointed at the dog, immediately a warrior rushed forward, picked up the dead dog and ran out of the room.

"Now that the dog has been taken care of, is there anyone in this room who wishes to test my patience?"

Aiden kept his gaze focused on the ground by

his feet, "I'm sure they get the point sir."

The Commander scowled, "Now to answer your question Alexi, only the crown royals can pass on their powers therefore I wish for them to be on my side of this war." The Commander started walking before the royals stopping in front of Marcus, "Of the crown royals I favored his daughter as she was the one with unusual powers, but it seems she resents me now. She'll never join me so she's better off dead."

"Don't go near-" Marcus started.

"I don't believe I was addressing you!" the Commander growled.

Juniper pulled the others away as to not be heard, "Carmine, Zane, Circe, Aanya, go find Aeolus, Diana, Victoria, and Hazel and make sure they're not hurt."

"What about you three?" Aanya whispered.

"We're going to see how these events unfold before doing anything else."

Juniper looked back into the room, to continue searching for the best course of action. Nothing happened during the next few minutes until Aiden slipped up and showed he knew something he shouldn't have.

Chapter 19

"So, tell me what am I doing here?" the strange man asked.

"Correct me if I'm wrong but your name is Samuel correct, and you have an older brother Sephtis?" the Commander asked.

"How did you know that?" Samuel asked.

"I make a point to know things about my targets."

Aiden looked up, "You said Sephtis, his brother?"

The Commander squinted suspiciously, "Yes I did, why do you sound so concerned by that?"

"It's just that," Aiden looked away, "The name sounded familiar."

The Commander forced Aiden to look up at him, "What do you know of that name?"

"Nothing, fath-" Aiden cut himself off by covering his mouth realizing the mistake too late.

"What were you about to say?" the Commander asked.

"Nothing sir," he responded quickly, moving

his hand away from his mouth.

"That didn't sound like nothing," The Commander lowered himself to eye level, "It almost sounded like you were about to say father."

"I-I didn't, I wasn't-" Aiden stammered.

The Commander reached forward and took something from the inside of Aiden's jacket, "Don't think for a second I didn't know you had this, I've seen you looking at its contents, but I've never known what's in here."

"It's not important."

"If it wasn't important I doubt you would have hidden it from me."

Aiden stepped back as the Commander opened the envelope. Aiden shot some fire at the paper and managed to light the ends.

"No!" The Commander shouted in rage, dropping the burning papers, "Pardon me, you really don't want me knowing what was in there."

"Why did I do that." Aiden muttered, looking at his shaking hands.

"You know something, I don't need those papers to know what you learned, all I need is your mind."

"What?"

The Commander reached his hand out toward Aiden, after a minute Aiden slumped forward and fell to the ground while the Commander had a small glowing orb floating in his hand. He looked at the glowing orb until an annoyed look swept across his face.

"Now I get it, you know who I am." He crushed the orb in his hand, "Not only do you know who I am now you know what I am to you."

Aiden looked up, "Is that why you've always 'favored' me?" he said putting air quotes on favored, "Is that why I'm your heir? Is that why you treated me so horribly?"

"Of course it is. You really think I wanted a disappointment for a son?"

Aiden struggled to his feet, "How come nothing I did was enough? My entire life all I wanted was to please you, make you proud of me."

"And what did that get you?"

"Scars covering my arms and following the orders of a horrible man out of fear for other people's lives."

The royals, support group, and Samuel's family watched in terror as the Commander slapped Aiden so hard that he fell over, "You should hold your tongue."

"I had PTSD at fourteen because of you!" Aiden shouted looking up at his father.

The Commander kicked Aiden in the face, then brought his foot down on his side with a sickening crack.

"I never wanted this life, I never wanted to be your son," Aiden continued.

Marcus pulled on his restraints, "Aiden stop it he'll kill you!"

"Tell me, who are you looking for..." Aiden paused, "Sephtis."

Samuel looked up, "What?"

The Commander stared daggers at his son, "Why you little-"

Sephtis kicked Aiden again, he struggled to his knees coughing up blood and his jaw out of place. Sephtis snapped his fingers and pointed at Aiden. Two warriors ran into the room, grabbed Aiden by either arm and dragged the half-conscious warrior away.

Sephtis pulled a knife from his pocket, "Now to punish whoever it was that gave him that information." He looked at the royals, his eyes landing on Alice, "She's not here right now but her family is, how do you suppose she's feeling about losing a mother?"

Juniper froze in fear, there wasn't time to get to her mother in time to save her. Juniper turned her head away from the scene and heard a loud scream.

"Erica!" Jason shouted from beside her.

Juniper looked at what was going on and saw Erica standing in front of Alice protecting her from the knife. Juniper leapt from her hiding place and caught Erica as she fell to the floor with a knife embedded in the very same spot her brother had been stabbed.

"No, no no no." Juniper cried, "I'm not losing you too."

"Oh well, that certainly looks familiar." Sephtis said with a smile, "Looks just like when Eylam died."

Juniper ignored Sephtis' comment, keeping her focus on her dying friend, "I'm not letting another Quinn die, you've only just met your family."

"I suppose this is karma for trying to kill you." Erica said with a laugh.

"Now's not the time for jokes." Juniper sobbed.

"If you couldn't save Eylam, you can't save me."

All the feelings Juniper had been pushing away came flooding back as Erica lay dying in her arms, the fear and anger from Aiden nearly killing her, the pain and grief from Eylam, regret from not speaking out about her reservations for the engagement. All this fear and pain shut down

Juniper's powers.

All the tension slipped from Erica and her body went limp, Juniper checked Erica's pulse. When she couldn't find one, she pressed her ear to Erica's chest. Juniper stood up leaving her friend laying still on the floor and faced her killer.

"What do you have against twins?"

Juniper took the hilt of her sword in her hand, she drew the blade and lunged forward swiping at Sephtis. Sephtis jumped backward dodging her blade. Juniper moved swiftly around him while he drew twin daggers and began an offense. The blades locked together; Juniper kicked Sephtis' leg causing him to lose his grip on his daggers.

Juniper held the tip of her sword to his throat, "You made a grave mistake targeting my friends and family."

"No princess, you made a mistake the moment you drew that sword for a fight."

Juniper saw movement out of the corner of her eye, she turned and felt searing pain in her arm, she looked down and saw a knife stuck in the left side of her collarbone.

Juniper heard a woman begin speaking, "In fact I get a bit angry when someone threatens the life of my husband."

Juniper dropped her sword and felt warm blood seeping down her arm and torso, "Don't come near me."

"Oh, dear girl, you're in no position to tell me what to do."

In a quick movement Juniper was on the floor with a foot pressed against her windpipe threatening to crush it. Juniper got a good look at her attacker's face, red eyes, dirty blonde hair and scars from targets who wouldn't go down without a fight.

"Well," Juniper coughed out, "It's nice to finally meet you, Kristen Blakely."

"Yes, it seems this is the meeting of a lifetime, my son with whom I've yet to have a conversation is locked in a cell screaming to get out and help you, my husband with an army able to take down the world, and you the princess who cannot bear to let others down"

Juniper struggled to remove the foot from her throat, "If you don't mind, I like breathing so please move your foot."

Kristen smiled, she picked up her food then brought it down on Juniper's face. Then she pulled the knife from her shoulder and drove into her side much too low to be fatal but still caused Juniper to scream and writhe in agony. Juniper fought to get to her feet when she heard a loud shout and saw Carmine standing in front of her face covered by his mask and his sword brandished. Zane slid to her side, his face covered in frost.

"Our friend." Zane said to Sephtis.

Sephtis glared at Zane, "Since when can you talk?"

Zane tapped his ear, "Hearing aids."

Juniper was slowly losing consciousness; she was supporting herself on her sword. The interactions between the warriors and Sephtis and Kristen became blurry. She knew there was a lot of shouting and sounds of blades clashing together.

Everything went dark for a split second and when Juniper managed to open her eyes, she found herself in Aiden's arms held tightly to his chest, feeling the blood continuing to seep down her side.

"I refuse to let you kill the only person who has ever shown me kindness," Aiden said.

"You can barely stand right now," Sephtis responded.

"I'll never continue following you, you'll never be my father," He spat.

Chapter 20

The last thing Juniper remembered hearing before losing consciousness completely was a gunshot, followed by a loud scream. When she came to, she woke up in a bright room with a heart monitor beeping next to her. She looked to her side and saw her father noticeably disheveled sitting quietly next to her and next to Marcus was her mother looking just as tired.

Juniper coughed, startling the two of them awake.

"Junie!" her mother cried.

"You're awake, finally." Marcus continued.

"What happened, is everyone okay?"

"Not entirely, Diana was fine, she did exactly what she was told, but Hazel froze up and got hit a few times resulting in a nasty bruise on her face, Victoria and Aeolus weren't so lucky." Marcus said gently.

"What happened to them?" Juniper begged.

Alice rubbed her arms, "We were told they put up a bit of a fight when it came to the warriors, both will make a full recovery, but both will have permanent scars and were discharged yesterday."

"What about the others, the warriors?" Juniper asked.

"Well, Jason is now half blind something stabbed his eye causing him to no longer be able to see with his right eye and will now need glasses, Zane sustained no physical injuries but did get frostbite, Aanya got two stab wounds in her shoulder and leg, Circe shifted to escape a group of them but they managed to clip her wings resulting in deep lacerations in her arms, and Carmine's throat got cut, not quite deep enough to be fatal but they said he's not allowed to talk for a few weeks," Alice explained, "We have been told all are expected to make a full recovery."

"Aiden was the worst of the group, a dislocated jaw, brocken eye socket, and a couple ribs, with two stab wounds. He unfortunately still has yet to wake up," Marcus said quietly.

Juniper lay in silence for a moment, "Wait what about Erica, was her body recovered?"

Marcus took a deep breath, "Yes but sadly she was not the only casualty."

Juniper froze, "What?"

Alice put a hand on her daughter's shoulder, "Sephtis if I'm remembering that name correctly, shouted about taking at least one of us and fired a gun, its bullet managed to find its target..." Alice paused, "In Prince Damian's chest."

"I suppose everything else is out in the open as well," Juniper muttered.

Marcus nodded, "Circe, Zane, and Aanya told us everything."

Juniper sat up, "There was one thing only Erica knew that I feel like I should also share."

"What?" asked Marcus.

"I know you think it's a good idea and it's what you all wanted of me but I can't keep it a secret anymore-" Juniper took a deep breath, "I don't want to marry Aeolus. I know there are benefits but the kingdoms already have good relations with each other and I just don't see Aeolus in that way. I'm sorry."

Alice took Juniper's hands, "Why are you apologizing? Did you think we'd be angry with you?"

Juniper sniffled a bit and nodded glumly.

Marcus looked surprised, "Oh Juniper, we're not mad. Actually believe it or not, Aeolus said almost the exact same thing, but he wasn't worried about what his family or we thought. He was worried that you would be upset."

"So if neither of us want-" Juniper started.

"Then the engagement is off, we don't want to force you two into a relationship you're not happy with nor can we force two people to feel a certain way about each other," Alice finished.

"Now about Aiden, Samuel after learning that his brother faked his death and then had a son, has refused to leave Aiden's side however neither have the police," Marcus whispered, "They're planning on arresting him as soon as he's recovered."

Juniper shook her head, "No he's worked too hard for his freedom, he's not a bad person he doesn't deserve that."

Marcus rubbed the back of his neck, "We know but we were waiting on your opinion because you know him the best out of everyone."

Juniper swung her legs off the bed, "Then we go tell them, I don't want him to go to prison. He'll get life, the only reason he sided with Sephtis is that that man threatened to kill people if he didn't."

"Junie don't get up, we'll call them in here, with a doctor," Marcus said, getting to his feet.

He began walking toward the door when Juniper said one more thing, "Hey dad."

"Yeah."

"You look like a hot mess."

Marcus turned to face his daughter, "Bold words from the one who almost died and has been unconscious for two days." He turned back to the door, "Besides it's not like Alice is any better."

Then Marcus left the room before Alice could come up with a good remark, Juniper turned to her mother, "Honestly mom what do you see in that man?"

Alice smirked, "I don't know."

Marcus came back with a police officer and a doctor. The doctor immediately walked over to Juniper and began going over her injuries while the police officer started asking questions.

"Apologies for my forwardness, Princess, but I've been told that you believe that young man who has assisted in holding all five royal families, a support group, and five other people hostage, injuring four including yourself, and killing two people, one of them being a prince, is a good person and should be pardoned."

"Well, when you say it like that it doesn't sound right but please hear me out," Juniper started, "Firstly I know this doesn't excuse what he has done but he was mentally, physically, and verbally abused his whole life causing him to follow the orders of a man he hated out of fear. Eventually he stopped caring about his own life; he believed he would rather be dead than doing what he was doing, however this resulted in other people getting killed when he disobeyed orders."

The police officer shook his head, "You're right, Princess that doesn't excuse his actions."

"Whether you want to believe it or not, by doing what he was doing he was saving more lives than if he had fought against what he was being told to do. In fact, if he had stopped, it's likely that his father would have succeeded in taking over the kingdoms as all of us would likely be dead." Juniper explained.

"He still aided in the deaths of that girl and Prince Damian," The officer argued.

"Hate to disagree with you but, when Erica, that girl, was killed he was not in the room and Erica took the knife of her own accord to save my mother, and when Damian was shot Aiden had sustained major injuries and two stab wounds, he had barely managed to save my life there was no possible way he could have gotten to his father to get the gun away from him to save Damian." Juniper continued, "He had nothing to do with those deaths."

"Princess, I don't mean to sound rude but even if he saved lives, two people still died," the officer shot back.

Juniper shook her head, "I just explained that he had nothing to do with that, and does the fact that royalty is vouching for him mean nothing?"

"He broke the law, Princess."

"And he saved my life, twice."

Marcus looked at her, "Twice?"

Juniper shook her head, "Later, it's a long story."

Marcus looked up at the cop, "Now that she has explained why she thinks that Aiden should be pardoned I will ask you, do you still believe he should go to prison?"

"Apologies, Your Majesty but, yes, he still broke the law," the officer said.

Marcus nodded, "Then I would like to pardon him."

"But Your Majesty-"

Marcus held up his hand, "I cannot speak for the other kingdoms and what they will say on the matter however as long as I'm here in Providence and he lives in my kingdom he has diplomatic immunity from all laws previously broken, should he commit these crimes again or break more laws he will be arrested but until that day he lives peacefully with my family as a guest in my kingdom," Marcus took a breath, "Is that clear?"

"Yes, I'm terribly sorry I will take my officers and go," the cop said with a bow.

The doctor finished looking over Juniper's injuries, "Well, Princess it seems your injuries have gotten far better. You should be good to go in a little while as long as you're careful and don't do anything crazy you'll be fine."

"Thank you," Juniper whispered. The doctor left the room and Juniper looked at her parents, "So where's the idiot who nearly got himself killed?"

Her mother shook her head and stood up, "Come on I think Samuel has some questions as well."

Juniper got up and followed her mother down the hall to Aiden's room. Juniper walked in hearing nothing but a heart monitor and quiet gentle breathing. She walked further in to see Aiden lying peacefully, his chest rising and falling slowly with bandages covering his arms and patches on his face for his jaw and eye socket. She looked past the bed and saw a man with coppery red hair and freckles covering his face. He looked up and Juniper saw his eyes, the same checkerboard as Sephtis.

"Princess Juniper!" he started, "I wasn't expecting to see you."

"It's alright you don't need to worry with formalities right now, it's Samuel, right?"

He nodded, "This boy called that man Sephtis, and said that he was his father, but please tell me, Princess was he talking about my brother or some other Sephtis?"

"Your brother faked his death, the Sephtis you

saw was your brother, this man here," Juniper said, gesturing to Aiden, "His name is Aiden Blakley-Kai, and he is your nephew."

"What's the most difficult for me to process right now is just that he said Sephtis was abusive toward him but the Sephtis I knew and grew up with was nothing but kind."

"I don't want to come off as rude, but unfortunately people change, sadly he changed for the worse."

"Also, he had a son? I'm just so confused."

Juniper felt bad for him, "That's understandable, suddenly being told your brother is alive and suddenly there's a new family member too. This is a ton of new information that you learned all at once."

Samuel looked at Aiden, "Is this guy, you said my nephew, a good person?"

Juniper looked at him, "One of the best I've ever met."

Juniper looked over her friend, gingerly she placed a hand on his jaw. Slowly she felt the bone pull back into place and repair itself. As she pulled away from Aiden he coughed, and his eyes fluttered open.

"Juni-per?" He croaked.

"Yeah, it's me."

He looked up at her for a moment then his

face went red, and he turned away, "Are you okay? Not too badly hurt?" he asked.

"Okay Aiden you were stabbed twice, and you just turned beet red," Juniper said.

"You were also stabbed twice, and me turning red was nothing."

"Yeah okay, anyway I have an important question," Juniper started, "The day before Eylam died he started a sentence about you after learning you were the one who almost killed me, he said, *'but I thought he-'* and cut himself off. Do you have any idea what he was about to say?"

Aiden glanced around, "I don't have a clue, do you have a guess?"

"Maybe, but only you would know the answer since he was talking about you after all."

"Umm excuse me, I hate to interrupt but if he's my nephew I'd like to chat with him for a bit," Samuel asked quietly.

"Yeah, that's fine." Juniper responded, "I should go anyway, see you later."

Aiden reached and grabbed Juniper's wrist, "Wait I have to ask."

"Hmm?"

"Because we crashed and ruined the wedding, are you and Aeolus rescheduling or-?"

Juniper shook her head, "As it turned out neither of us wanted to marry the other. I kept my feelings to myself as I was scared of disappointing my parents, and he hid his because he was scared of disappointing me and ruining our friendship."

Aiden struggled to sit up, "So what does that mean for the engagement?"

"It's off we're not getting married."

Aiden nodded, "Okay that's all I wanted to know."

Juniper turned to leave, she walked back down the hall to her room. She entered her room to see the doctor waiting for her.

"Okay so we've gone over everything and since you appear to be walking around just fine." he said going over his clipboard, "you are free to go back to Flora."

"Thank you."

"But if you suddenly feel sharp pain or anything that may be cause for alarm, or of course your stitches pop please go to your nearest hospital immediately."

"I will thank you for all your help, and Aiden Blakley-Kai in the room two doors down the hall is awake."

"Great, well I believe your parents are waiting for you downstairs, so, Princess if you are ready you can change, they brought clothes for you, and head out."

Juniper nodded and the doctor left. Juniper

changed into the clothes her parents had for her and walked down to them. She joined her parents in the lobby then they returned to their palace where she could finally think about everything that had happened.

As Juniper paced her room all the feelings she had pushed away and the thoughts she swallowed came free and she let them freely into her mind. Juniper knew that keeping her opinions hidden and not telling anyone what was going on is what made everything more difficult. Juniper took a breath and came to terms with everything she thought then turned her mind to Erica and Eylam.

"They deserve a proper funeral," she whispered to herself.

Juniper pulled out her phone and found Celeste's number.

'I know this is short notice, but I want to hold a small memorial service for your children ASAP, Eylam never got a proper send off, and we won't be able to retrieve his body, but I do have the knife that killed him and his glasses. Let me know what you think when you can.'

Juniper sent the text then walked to Erica's room. She looked around for Eylam's knife and his glasses hoping Erica didn't keep them on her. She opened several drawers until getting to the nightstand, she opened the small door on the front and saw a sheathed knife next to a glasses case.

Juniper took the case and opened it, "Good they're here."

Juniper removed the knife from the nightstand, she got up to leave and ran into her father, "Juniper what are you doing?"

"Dad, well these belonged to Eylam, well the glasses did. This was the knife that killed him. Erica kept these things and we managed to recover her body and I wanted to hold a very small memorial for them, so I needed these things."

Marcus looked at the knife and glasses, "I was already planning on at least burying Erica with her family there, if we could find them, so her body is already at a funeral home."

"That's fine I mean we managed to find all of their families, they're all part of the same support group so a small thing with just them and the others, so just like a burial and-" Juniper's voice caught and she wiped tears from her eyes, "-they just need something nice."

"Junie, I need you to listen for a second, after what happened and in light of all this new information, there isn't going to be a service for Damian."

Juniper stopped, "What?"

"It's understandable, after Sephtis getting away with Kristen, and what happened with you they just don't want to risk it." Marcus explained, "Victoria is already injured, Lucas isn't okay emotionally, and Timothy and Lacy just lost one of their sons."

"That makes perfect sense." Juniper looked at what she was holding, "I still want a small private thing for Erica and Eylam, they both died for this, and Erica saved mom's life."

Marcus pulled his daughter into a hug, "I know, I never met Eylam but the way you and your friends talk about him it's clear all of you thought highly of him."

Juniper broke down, "They both need recognition for their actions, they were some of the kindest people I've ever met. If it weren't for Eylam I'd be dead."

"Hang on, I thought you said Jason saved you after you were nearly killed?"

"Eylam is the one who found me and got me to Jason in time."

"Well, I'll make sure people know what those two have done, they are heroes."

Juniper nodded and spent the next few days working with the support group to organize a funeral for Erica and Eylam. Jason was the first released from the hospital with a prescription for new glasses, Zane and Carmine were let out at the same time, Zane was told to stay warm for a while and Carmine was told to be careful of foods that could be too hot to eat. Circe was let out two days later with her arms now tightly bandaged instead of in casts and the following day Aanya got to leave on crutches being told to stay off her left leg because her hip made it difficult and painful to use, while her shoulder was almost completely recovered.

"So, about this memorial for Erica and Eylam?" Jason started going over what Juniper had given him.

"It's tomorrow, just a burial service and a small local funeral home." Juniper said, pointing toward the bottom of the paper.

Circe rubbed her arms, "And who's going to be there?"

"Aiden is getting discharged today, so him, us, and the support group."

Carmine nodded, "That seems to be everything, the coffins are ready, Erica's body is prepared, Eylam's glasses and knife are set in place, and the flowers-"

Aanya looked up from her papers, "Gathered and ready."

Juniper set her papers down, "Well everything seems to be in order, now I'm heading down to get Aiden, he doesn't have a ride here."

Juniper stood up and walked down to the doors of the palace requesting a driver from one of the maids as she walked. Juniper stood patiently at the front doors of the palace for the car to pull up after swinging by her room to grab something for Aiden.

As Juniper got in, she looked at the driver, "Providence central hospital please."

"Your wounds bothering you, Your Highness?" the driver asked, starting to drive away.

"No, just picking up a friend."

Juniper sat quietly in the car on the two-hour ride. As the car pulled up to the doors she glanced to the side. Juniper got out of the car and walked into the building. She stood quietly in the waiting room for Aiden to come down holding a small bag behind her back.

Aiden walked into the waiting room with a doctor to tell him a few things before Aiden turned and saw Juniper, "Well look who's come to pick me up."

Juniper held the bag out at arm's length, "I got you something, and don't think you're special I got one for the others as well."

Aiden took the bag, "What is it?"

"Well, when we get back to the palace and you

go into your room, there's a new properly tailored wardrobe for you using the measurements of your old uniform and new fighting clothes I figured you'd need them, as for what's in that bag-"

Aiden reached into the bag and pulled out a small box, "You got me a cell phone?"

"Again, figured you'd need one, now that you have freedom, you'll need to stay up to date on what's going on and be able to easily communicate with others."

"Well thank you, Juniper."

"Don't feel too special like I said the others got the exact same thing."

The two of them left the hospital and returned to the Flora palace.

Chapter 21

The next morning all of the warriors headed down to the funeral home. The seven of them met up with the support group and together carried two coffins out to their final resting place, one holding Erica and the other containing nothing but a pair of glasses and a knife. As the group lowered the coffins into the ground and stepped away, Juniper held out her hands and steadily used vines to move the soil filling the graves. Jason and Aiden stepped forward with two bouquets of roses, both had the black and white roses.

Juniper looked at the roses laying on the graves and took a quivering breath, "Today is a sad day, and I'm truly sorry Eylam could never be reunited with his family and Erica lost her life not even a week after finally seeing them again. They are both heroes, Eylam having saved my life and Erica saving my mother's, despite everything they made a found family of friends and became some of the most amazing people I've ever met."

Aiden cleared his throat, "I feel I'm partially responsible for both of these deaths, I was there and watched as Eylam died when I could have easily taken him to get help instead I froze in fear; and if I hadn't made that mistake Alice's life wouldn't have been in danger and Erica would never have taken that knife." he wiped tears from his eyes, "I'm truly and forever sorry to the two of them."

Juniper looked at the group silently asking if anyone else wanted to say anything, when nobody did, she looked down, "I truly hope the two of these amazing people will be remembered if not by us then by what they've done for us."

After the funeral everyone returned home. Juniper was sitting in her room reading a book when someone knocked on her door, she got up and answered her door to Aiden.

"Need something?" Juniper asked.

Aiden looked at her and took a deep breath, "I'msorryIknowthattheengagement wascalledoffandyouprobablydon'tthinkof- hethesamewaybutIlikeyouandwhenIwoke upandsawyoumyfirstthoughtwasshe'sprettiert- hanasunflower."

"Woah slow down, I didn't understand a word you just said."

"Okay you want to know why I turned beet

red when I woke up?"

Juniper nodded, "Yeah."

Aiden laughed, "Okay this is really embarrassing but, when I saw you after waking up the first thing that came to mind was 'she's prettier than a sunflower'."

Juniper felt her face go red, "Are sunflowers in your opinion the prettiest kind of flower?"

He shrugged, "Yeah they are, I mean I've always kinda hated roses."

"Aiden answer me truthfully this time, when Eylam said *'but I thought he-'* was the rest of that sentence *'had a crush on you'*?"

Aiden stumbled over his words, "Well it's just you're pretty. A-and you're the only person who treated me with kindness. You just-" he turned away from her, his face beet red, "Was it that obvious?"

"I think I was too busy repressing my feelings and emotions about you that I didn't notice."

"What kind of feelings were you repressing?"

Juniper laughed in embarrassment, "Promise you won't laugh at me?"

"Promise."

"At one point I looked at you and thought you were really sweet and if I had to come up with an analogy, I'd have to say I think you're sweeter than a cinnamon bun."

Aiden looked at her, his face redder than his eyes, "I don't know what to say to that."

"Try nothing, just don't say a word."

He looked at her confused, before she grabbed his shirt collar and pulled him down into a kiss. He stood surprised for a moment before he wrapped his arms around her waist. The moment was ruined when they heard slow clapping down the hall.

"Well, it's about time." Jason said, grabbing their attention, "That took way too long."

Aiden stepped toward him angrily, "I'm going to kill you, Jason."

Jason spun around on his heel and took off down that hall, Aiden was about to chase after him when Juniper grabbed his wrist and pulled him into another kiss. She felt time had stood still and wanted to stay like this forever but knew the war was far from over.

"Hey Aiden, let's put the fact that Sephtis escaped and is still out there aside for a while and live in peace?"

"I like the sound of that."

Epilogue

Aiden stood next to Juniper looking at the old university campus, "Sunflower, what are we doing here?"

"Well, it's been a few months since everything happened, Carmine is picking up speed with his music and recently auditioned for a movie, Circe is at the police academy, Zane is taking speech lessons while he and Aanya are now enrolled in high school, and Jason recently got into the best medical school in the kingdom." Juniper explained

"That doesn't answer my question."

"Well, Cinnabon, soon enough Sephtis is going to start sending warriors our way and we need to be ready for them with a new place to stay."

Aiden looked around and walked up to the fountain, "So we're going to set this place up for them to live here?"

Juniper nodded, "It closed this last year so the only thing we really need to do is clean up."

He walked further across the quad, "I suppose it's doable."

Juniper took her boyfriend's hand, "You know we can't let him continue using these innocent teenagers for his selfish purposes, and they can't go back into normal society immediately."

"Yeah, this'll work,"

The two of them walked through the buildings and looked at the scenery. They were standing out on an old soccer field when Juniper's phone rang.

"Hello?"

"Hey Junie." said a voice on the other line.

"Oh, Carmine what's going on?"

"I've got some news."

"Oh really?"

"Yeah, I got the lead in that movie and filming starts next month."

Juniper smiled, "That's awesome I'll let Aiden know, see you later."

Juniper hung up and tucked her phone back into her purse and walked over to Aiden who was admiring an overgrown garden.

"Hey Sunflower, who was that on the phone?

"Oh, it was Carmine, he got the lead in that movie."

Aiden nodded, "Good for him, "

"Yeah, so what do you think of this place as

The Facility 2.0?"

Aiden smiled while picking a flower from the garden, "I think it's perfect."

He tucked the flower behind Juniper's ear and took her hand. They both turned and left the university, got into the car and drove back to the Flora palace.